How We End.

Stories by
Hannah Schneider

Images by
Kate Stone

Copyright © 2015 Hannah Schneider and Kate Stone

Photographs © Kate Stone

All rights reserved.

First Edition

ISBN-10: 0692534733

ISBN-13: 978-0-692-53473-1

This is a work of fiction. Names, characters, businesses, places, events and incidents are either the products of the author's imagination or used in a fictitious manner. Any resemblance to actual persons, living or dead, or actual events is purely coincidental.

Designed by Margot Laborde

HowWeEndBook.com

For the ones who brought us home.

Contents

Foreword	1
Daniel	7
Mason	11
Hudson	15
Spencer	19
Conor	23
Henry	27
Brandon	33
Pascal	37
Ray	41
Jimmy	45
Patrick	49
Kyle	53
Lee	57
Naomi	63
Kyle, again	67
Sam	71
Jack	75
Tony	79
Greg	83
Bennett	89
Charlie	95
Milo	99
Durant	105
Scott	109
Will	113
Durant, again	117
Nikolai	121
John	127
Carlos	131
Mike	135
Lukas	139
Will, again	145
Gunner	149
James	153
Adam	157
Caleb	161
Owen	165
Sam, again	169
Chase	173
Asher	177
Theo	181

Foreword

It starts with a need to understand. You need to make sense of it for yourself, but also for others. How do you explain what went wrong? Which moments sum up a relationship? You tell the story once and it becomes just that—a story. Sometimes you do it to make yourself feel better, or look better. Other times, you're more honest about how it went. Depends on who you're telling. Depends on whether you want to hurt someone. Depends on whether you're hurt. Sometimes it didn't hurt at all. Sometimes it was just funny. Those stories are usually the easiest to tell because you're not worried about facts—you just want the punch line to land.

You sit around with your girlfriends, or your aunt and uncle at that Italian place uptown, or the woman who threads your eyebrows, and you start the story. You include more or fewer details, but some pieces always fall right into place—the stupid shirt that he always wore, the sesame seed stuck in your teeth the entire time, the alcohol that you'd had too much of. These things feel integral, but you're not sure why. They don't explain how you grew apart, but they consumed you in the moment. They are the things you cannot shake. They are the details that you come back to when you're telling the story for the third time in a single night because everyone wants to know why you came alone.

You tell the story as clearly and as truly as you can, knowing it will never be quite right. You're not remembering it as it was. When you mention the ugly sofa in his apartment, you realize that each person you tell will imagine their own ugly sofa and none of them will be the one. They are not picturing that same green velvet. They cannot know about the coffee stain on the center cushion or the scratches in the dark wooden legs, where his cat sharpened its claws. You forget to mention the cat entirely. You want to stick to the most salient details, but every time you repeat the story, a gap opens up between you and the person you're telling. Telling the story is supposed to close the distance between you and the other person, but instead the gulf widens, because as they listen, they are creating their own version of things and it will never match yours. The relationships feel like small rooms in your mind that no one else will ever be able to walk into. Your audience begins to doubt you. They know you're leaving things out. They suspect that you are difficult, and they may be right. You falter, scrapbooking sweet moments from earlier in the relationship, wanting to prove that you are lovable. You begin to suspect that you're not, but you keep telling the story anyway.

One night, after a strange one, you tell the man at the bodega who sells expired milk. It's your own fault for never checking the date and so you never blame him. Instead, you start in about the latest disaster. It's a funny one, and he laughs at the right parts, which feels good. There is a language barrier and he clearly doesn't understand why you're so comfortable telling him a story that involves a broken condom, but you tell it to the end and then shove the entire carton of milk in your purse.

On the walk home, you imagine yourself as a small, unstable island, bobbing down the sidewalk. You begin to make peace with the fact that communication is imperfect. Even if it's all a waste of breath, you can't stop trying. If all you can do is present a sort of funhouse mirror view, you will at least do that. You need to keep trying to close those gaps, otherwise the emptiness becomes cavernous and you start to drown in those little rooms.

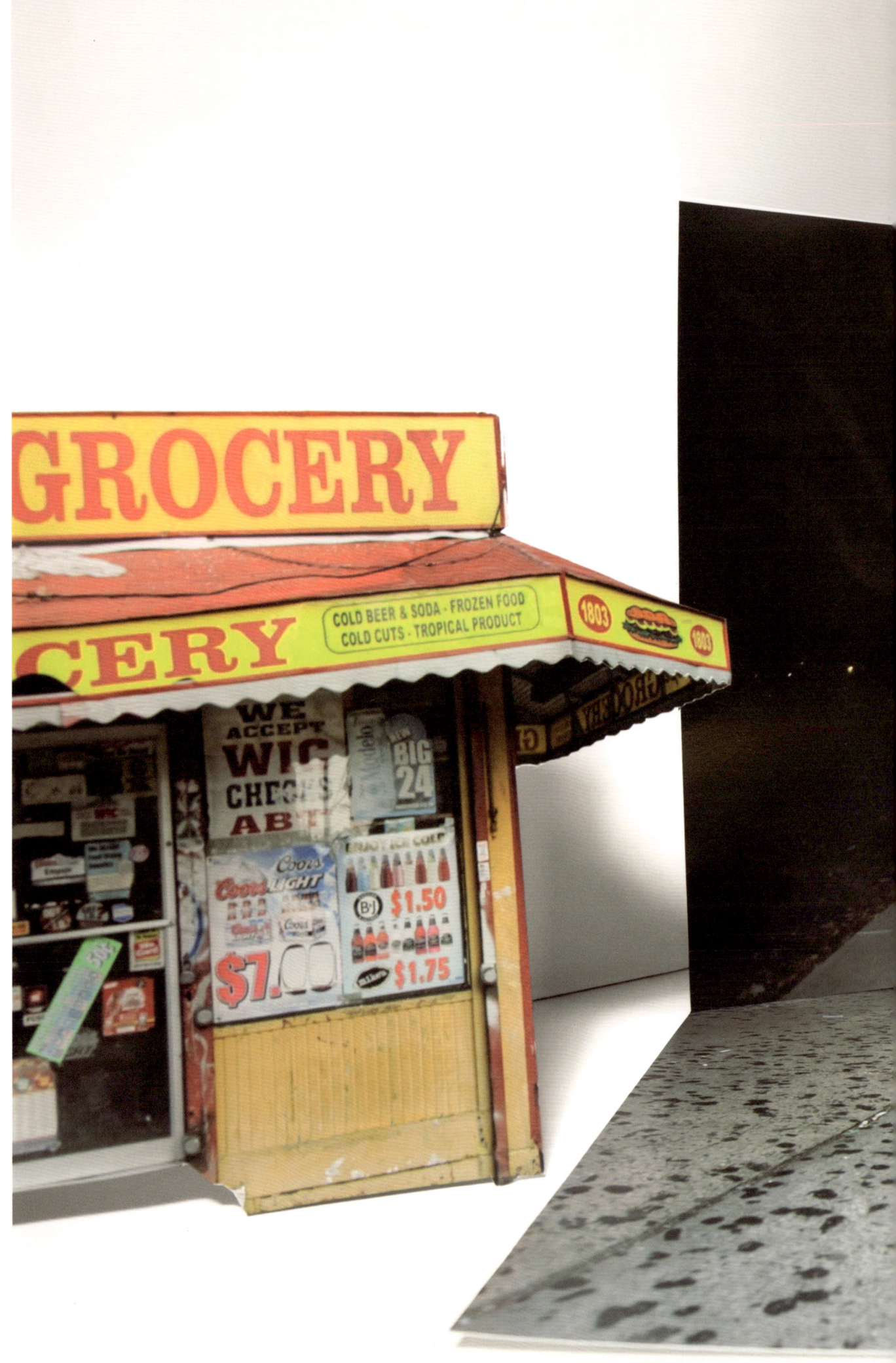

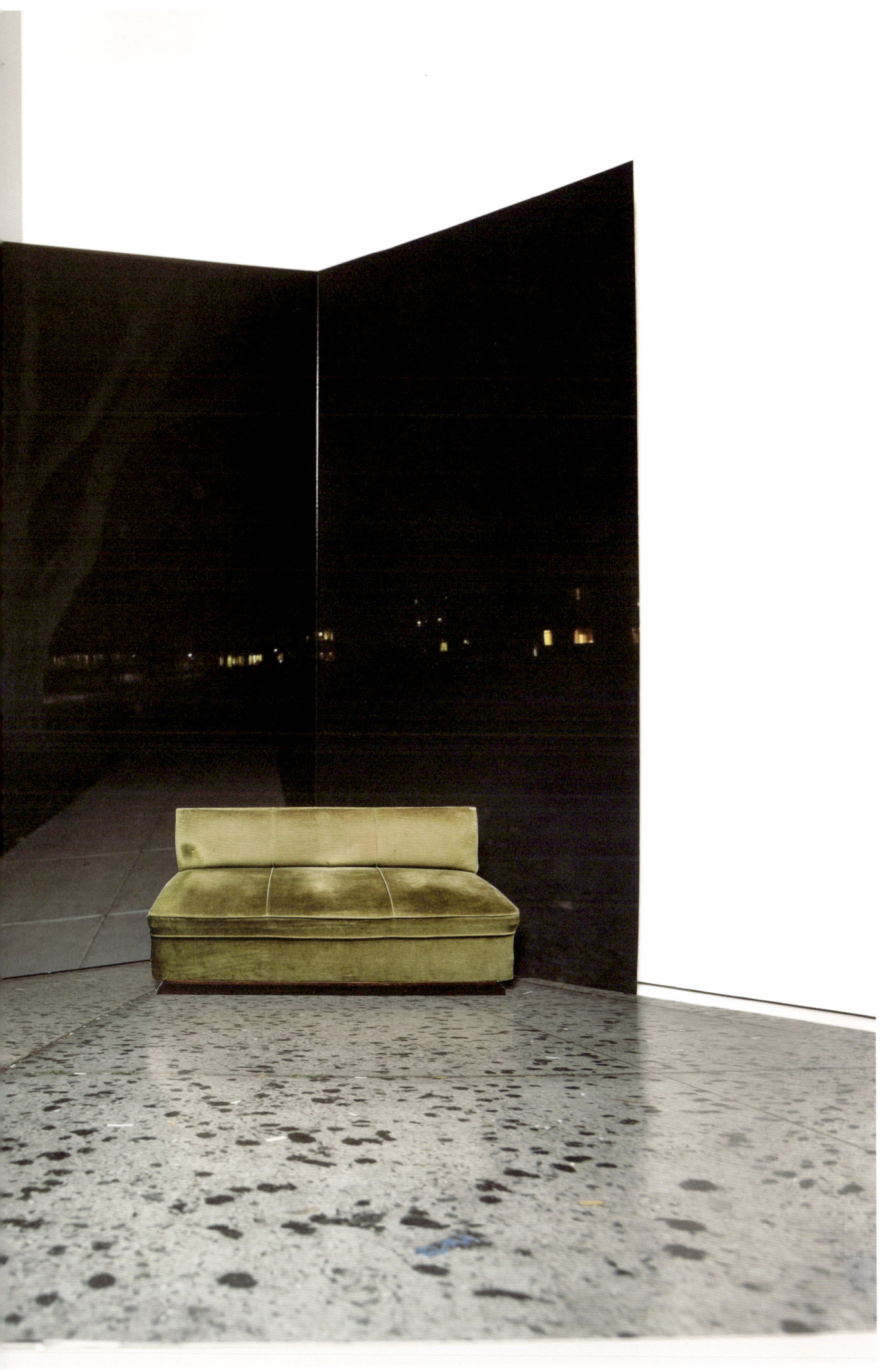

Daniel

Daniel was an accidental boyfriend. He pulled me behind the wall on the handball courts and told me that his parents were making him move to Staten Island. *I'm sorry*, I said. *It'll be all right.* Aping behavior that I'd seen in movies, I wrapped my arms loosely around him and we stood like that, listening to the *thump, thump, thump* of blue handballs hitting the other side of the wall.

He called me that night and, when I asked why, he said, *Because you're my girlfriend now, right?* I should've told him right then that he was mistaken. I couldn't though, because I was convinced that it was my own fault for attempting to project an older, wiser version of myself. I felt as though I'd deceived him and, in the end, it felt kinder to tell him that I was sorry, *but I can't date anyone from Staten Island.*

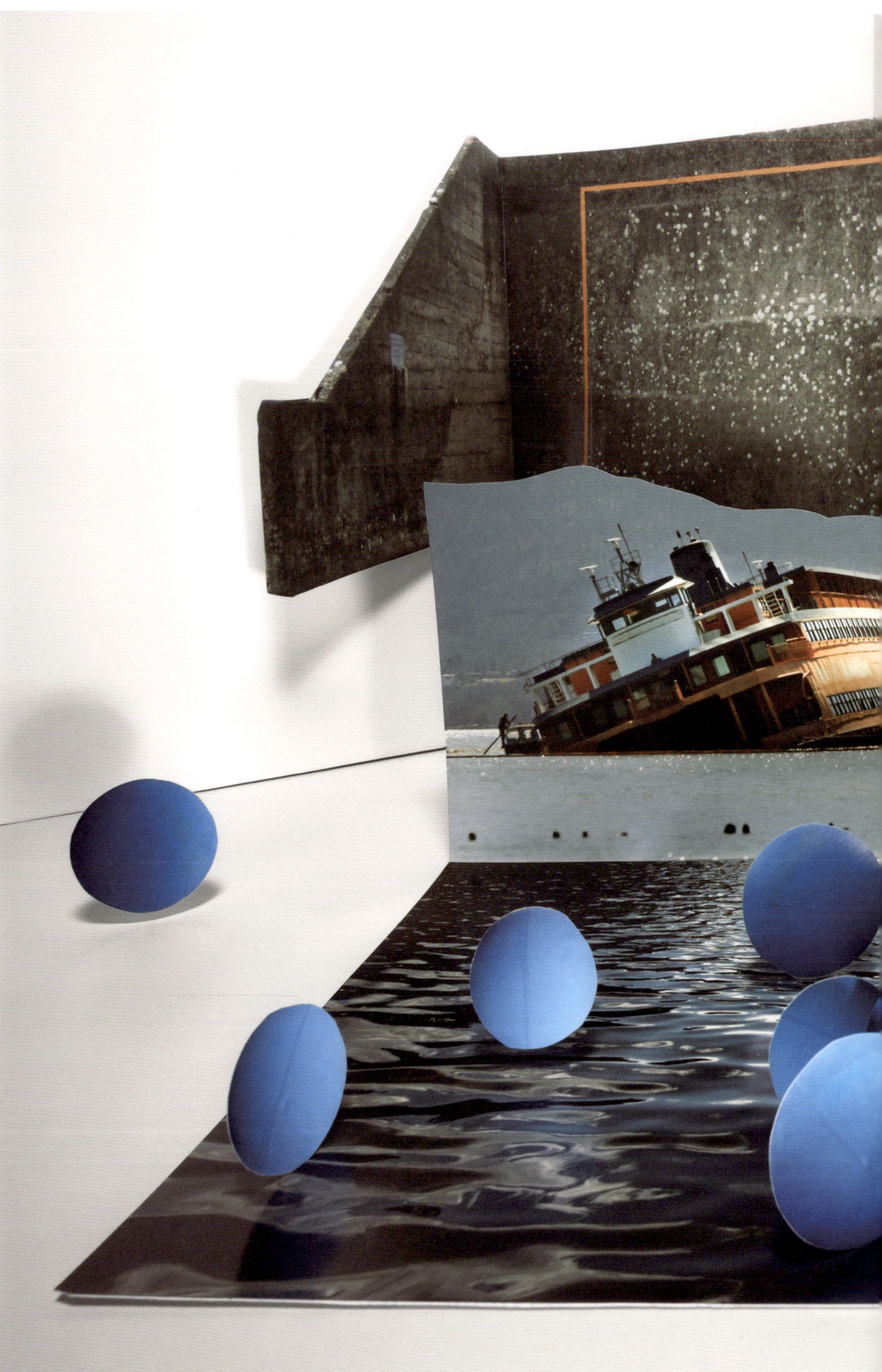

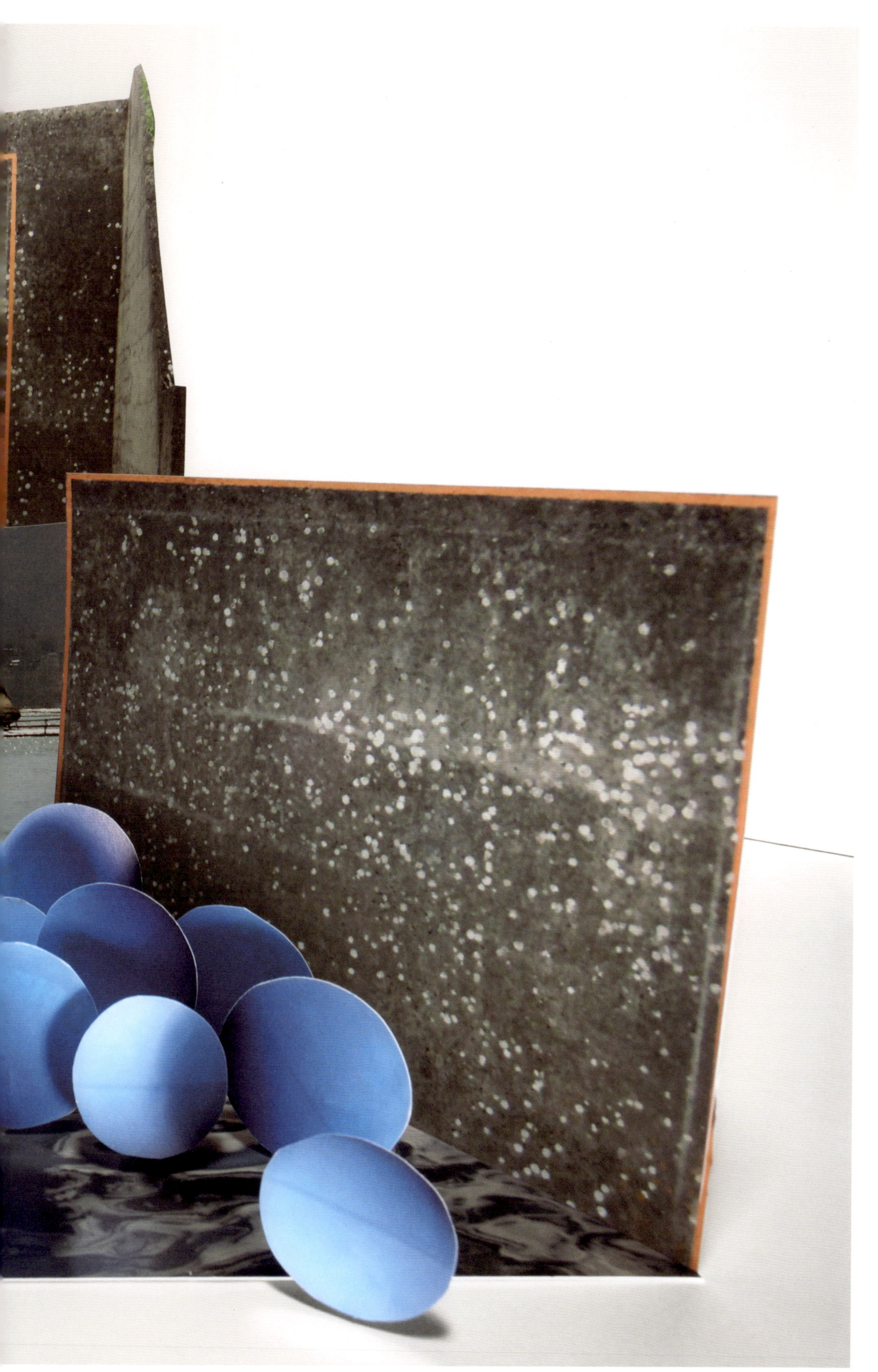

~~Daniel~~
Mason

Mason would come over after school to do homework on Wednesdays, because no one else was home. We would kiss goodbye, but not much more than that. Mostly it was just the thrill of being alone together. I liked the way his shoes looked, next to mine, by the front door.

It was October and we were chasing my cat around the kitchen island. I don't remember what it was exactly, but I remember laughing so hard that my throat was raw. We both had our socks on, running full speed in circles on the clean tiles. I slipped by the window and fell. I didn't catch myself or break my fall. I landed hard, on my back. I didn't cry because I couldn't catch my breath at first. Mason came over and helped me up. We laughed about it, or I tried to, but I didn't want to look at him. He didn't seem to think twice about it, once he realized that I was all right, but my embarrassment was a thick, nauseating thing that I couldn't get out of. I never wanted to see him again.

I ignored him for the next two days, which was all it took to shake him.

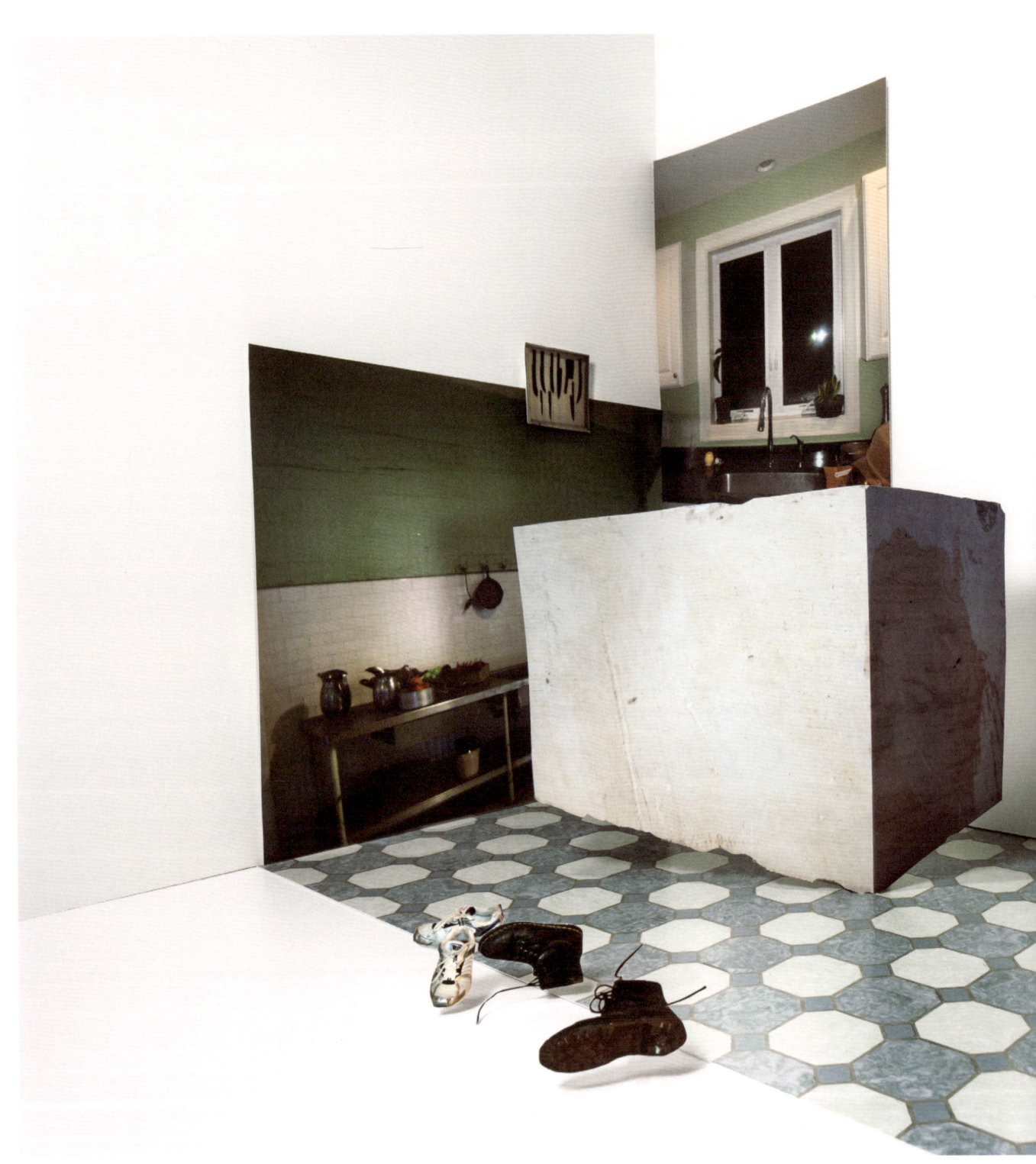

~~Daniel~~
~~Mason~~
Hudson

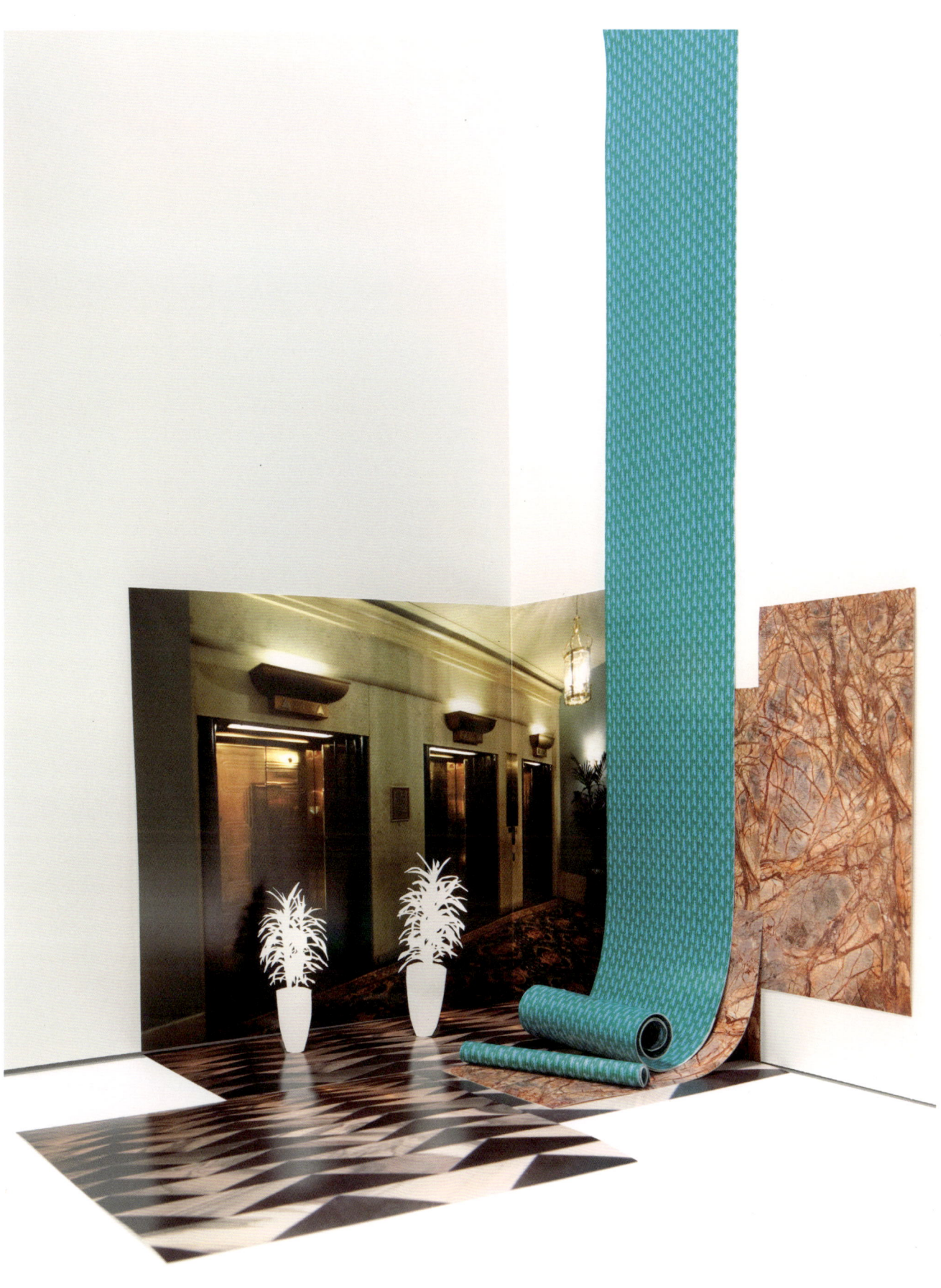

We were in front of elevators, which is a terrible place to talk about anything. I worried the whole time about the doors opening. The *whole time* was probably between three and five minutes, because that's how long it took Hudson to say that he was sorry and that maybe we could try to be a couple again, *later*.

I let him say his part. I didn't interrupt and I didn't argue. When he was done, I handed him a gift that I'd originally planned on giving him for his birthday, two weeks from then.

Whoa, he said. *I've never gotten a breakup present before. That's kinda cool.*

Yeah, I said. *I'm fucking awesome, huh?*

Yeah, he said. *Shit.*

~~Daniel~~
~~Mason~~
Hudson
Spencer

I had terrible insomnia, but Spencer would stay up with me, on the phone, and play quiet lullabies on his guitar. The songs were beautiful and when I asked where he'd learned them, he told me that he'd written them. *For you*, he said. Spencer had dated my best friend for exactly twenty-five days, which was enough to make him off limits, but I couldn't unhear the way he'd said it—*for you*.

The first time we kissed, we were supposed to be studying for a standardized test. I pretended to be surprised by the whole thing, but the truth is that I was ready for it. Spencer was the reason that I'd put a lock on my door. The first time that I latched it shut and turned around to see him waiting on my bed, my stomach dropped. I knew it was over from the moment we started. His tongue tasted like salt and I immediately hated the idea that I couldn't tell my best friend about it.

Two years later, my best friend lost her virginity to Spencer in my basement, at a New Year's party. I never did tell her about kissing him, but we grew apart anyway.

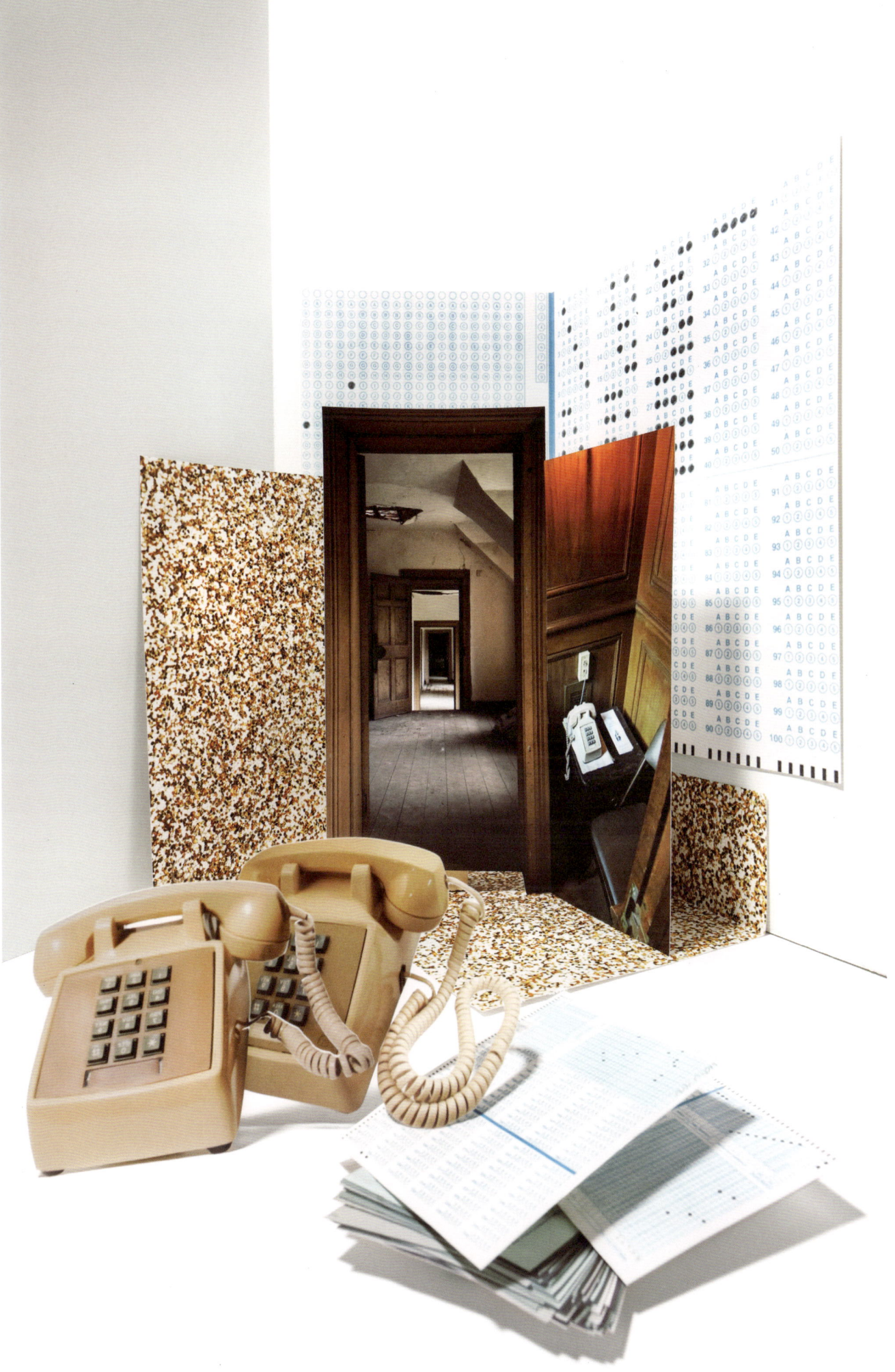

~~Daniel~~
~~Mason~~
~~Hudson~~
~~Spencer~~

Conor

I was a virgin.

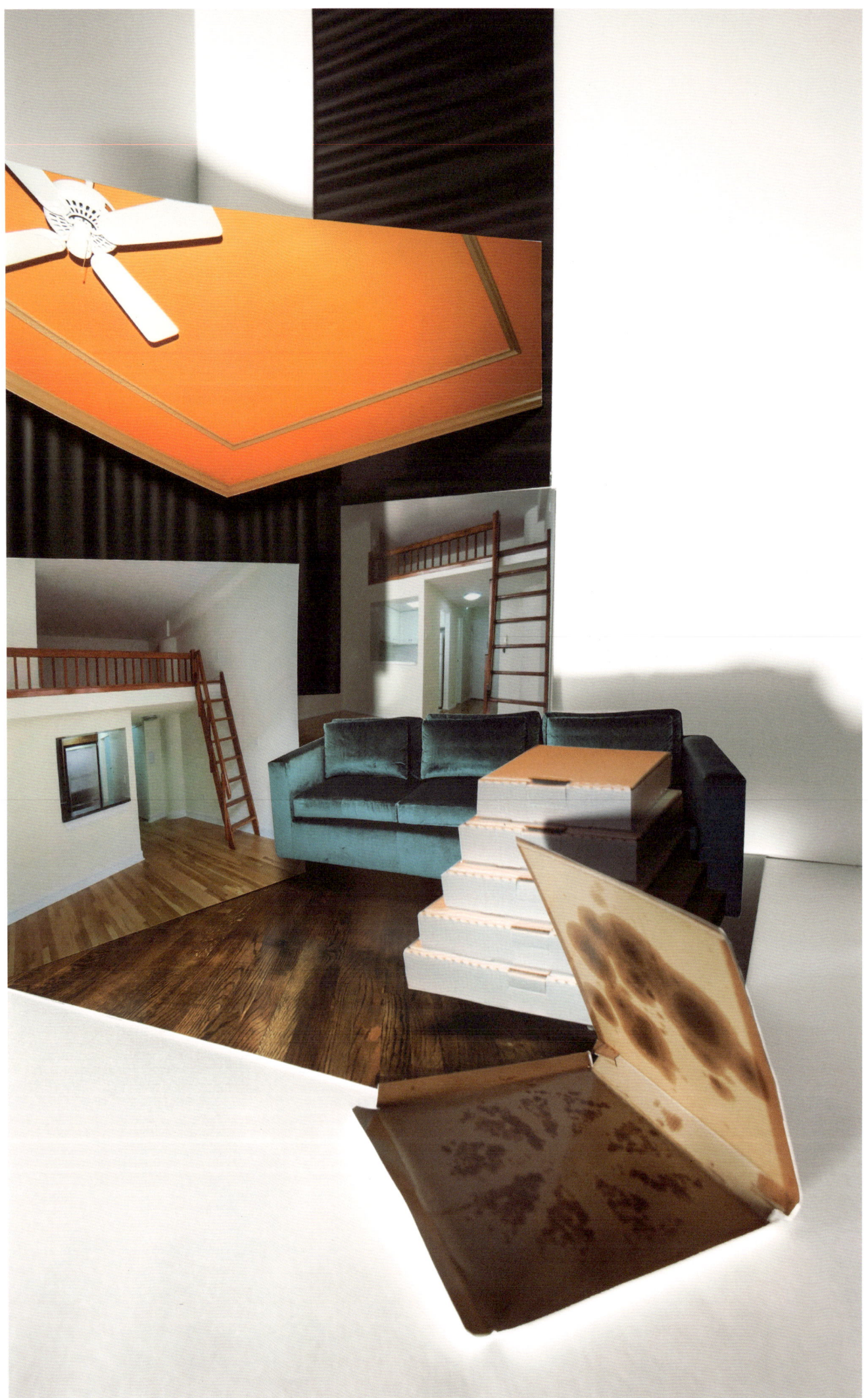

Conor invited me to spend the weekend at his apartment, while his parents were out of town. He ordered a pizza, but I could barely eat. I couldn't figure out what to do with my arms and legs. Every position I put myself in seemed completely absurd. I felt better after he kissed me, because he arranged me underneath him.

I needed to tell him that I was a virgin. I wasn't trying to shut things down between us, but that was the message I sent. If I'd been able to talk to him about it at all, we could have gotten past it, but my throat just closed up.

The sight of Conor pulling his jeans up gutted me.

~~Daniel~~
~~Mason~~
Hudson
Spencer
~~Conor~~

Henry

~~Daniel~~
~~Mason~~
Hudson
Spencer
~~Conor~~

Henry and I didn't stop loving each other for a long time. Once a year, he would show up at my doorstep with vodka, which we'd drink out of juice glasses. We were both dating other people who we never told about those nights. *You really loved me, didn't you?* I would ask and he would nod and say, *Yes*.

I can't wait to cheat on my wife with you, he would say and I would smile, knowing full well that we deserved each other.

Nothing much would happen, even though we set ourselves up for it every time. I was always sure to drink enough so that no one could have blamed me. Him maybe, but not me.
I did it on purpose, but it almost always ended the same way: I walked Henry to the front door and we stood there too long.

I don't like this. It's just like breaking up over and over.

We have to, he said. *Otherwise it won't stick.*

You're a real asshole, I said.

Good girl, he said, kissing my neck.

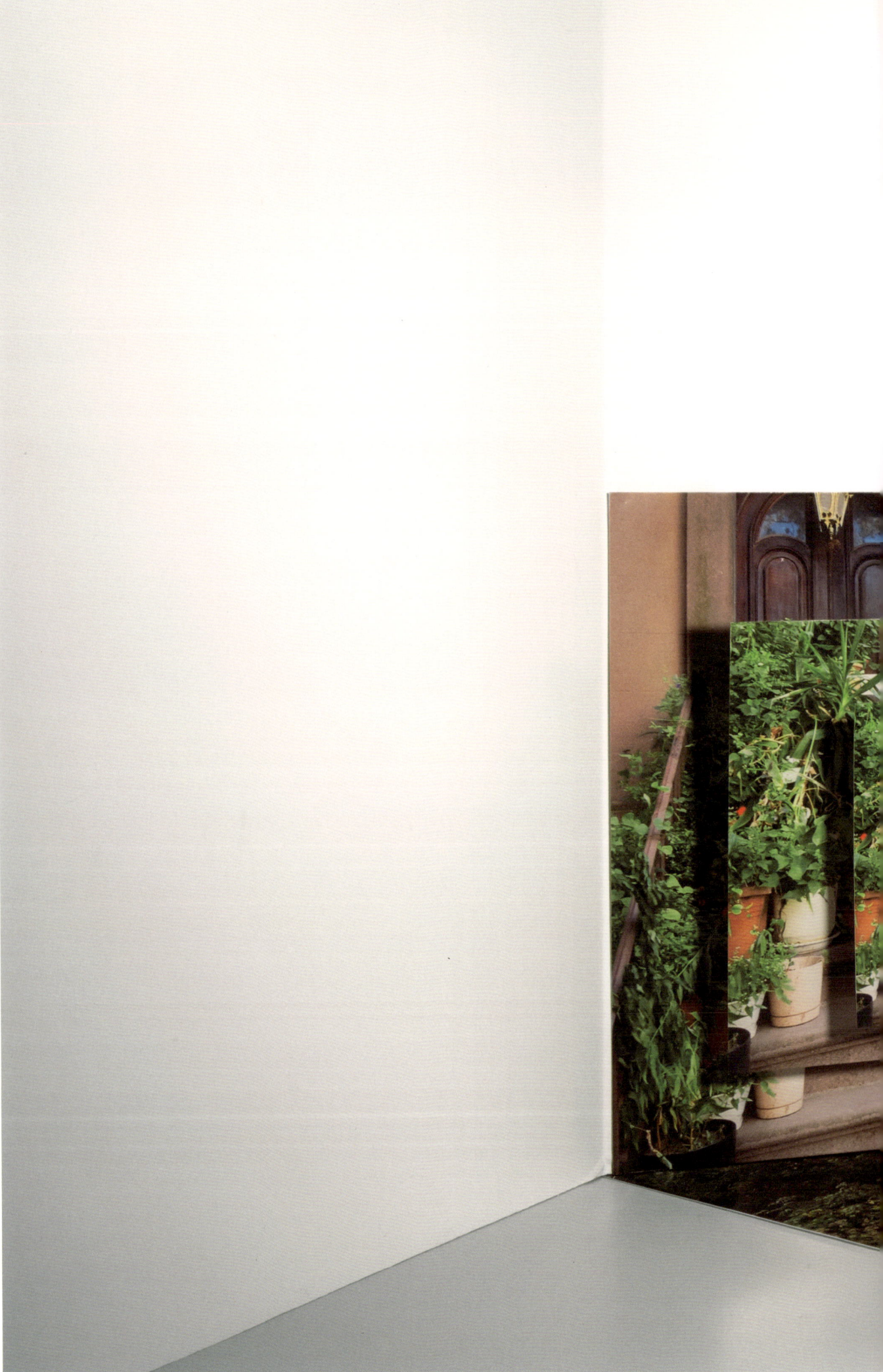

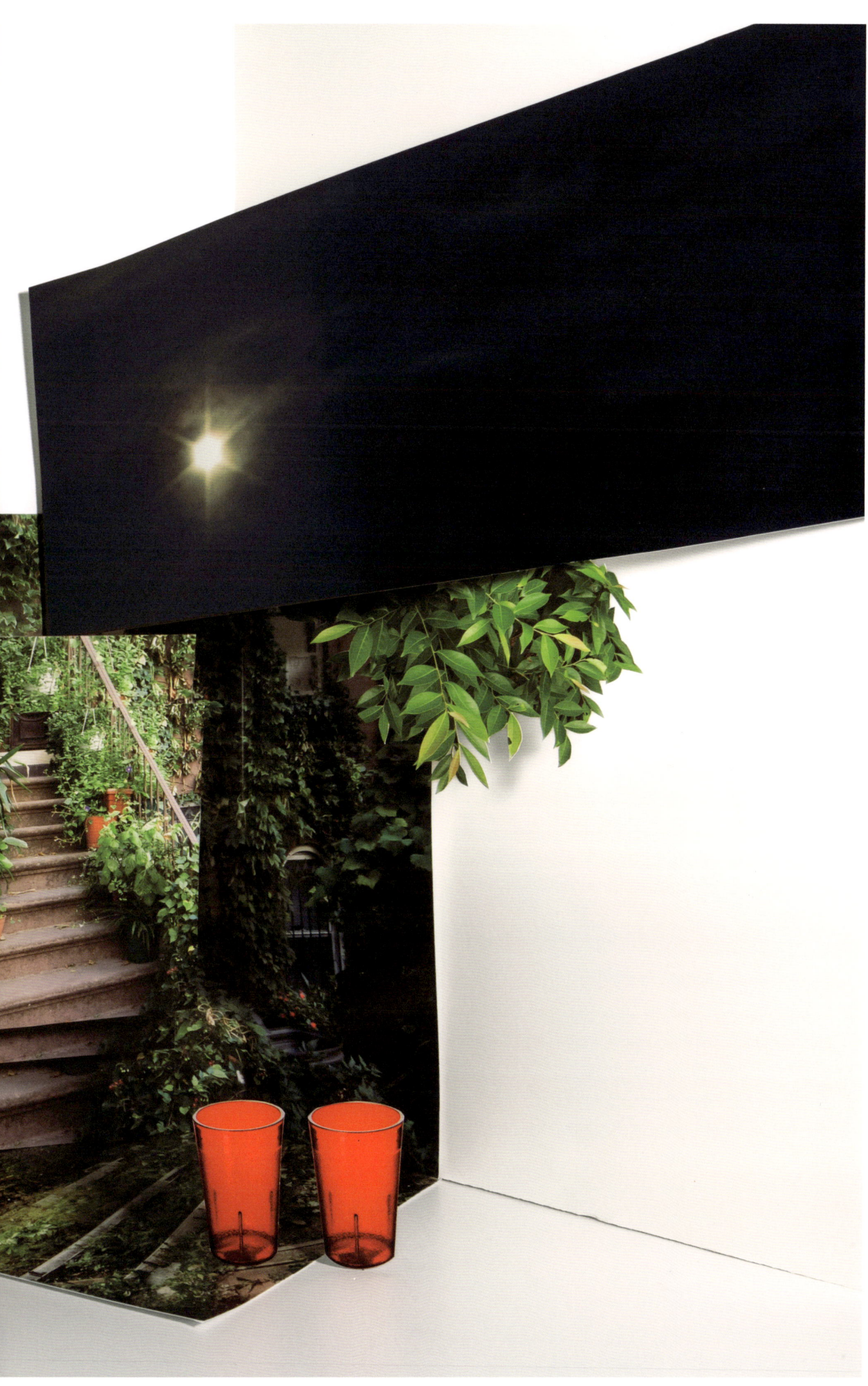

I can'
to c
on my
with

wait
eat
wife
you.

~~Daniel~~
~~Mason~~
~~Hudson~~
~~Spencer~~
~~Conor~~
~~Henry~~
Brandon

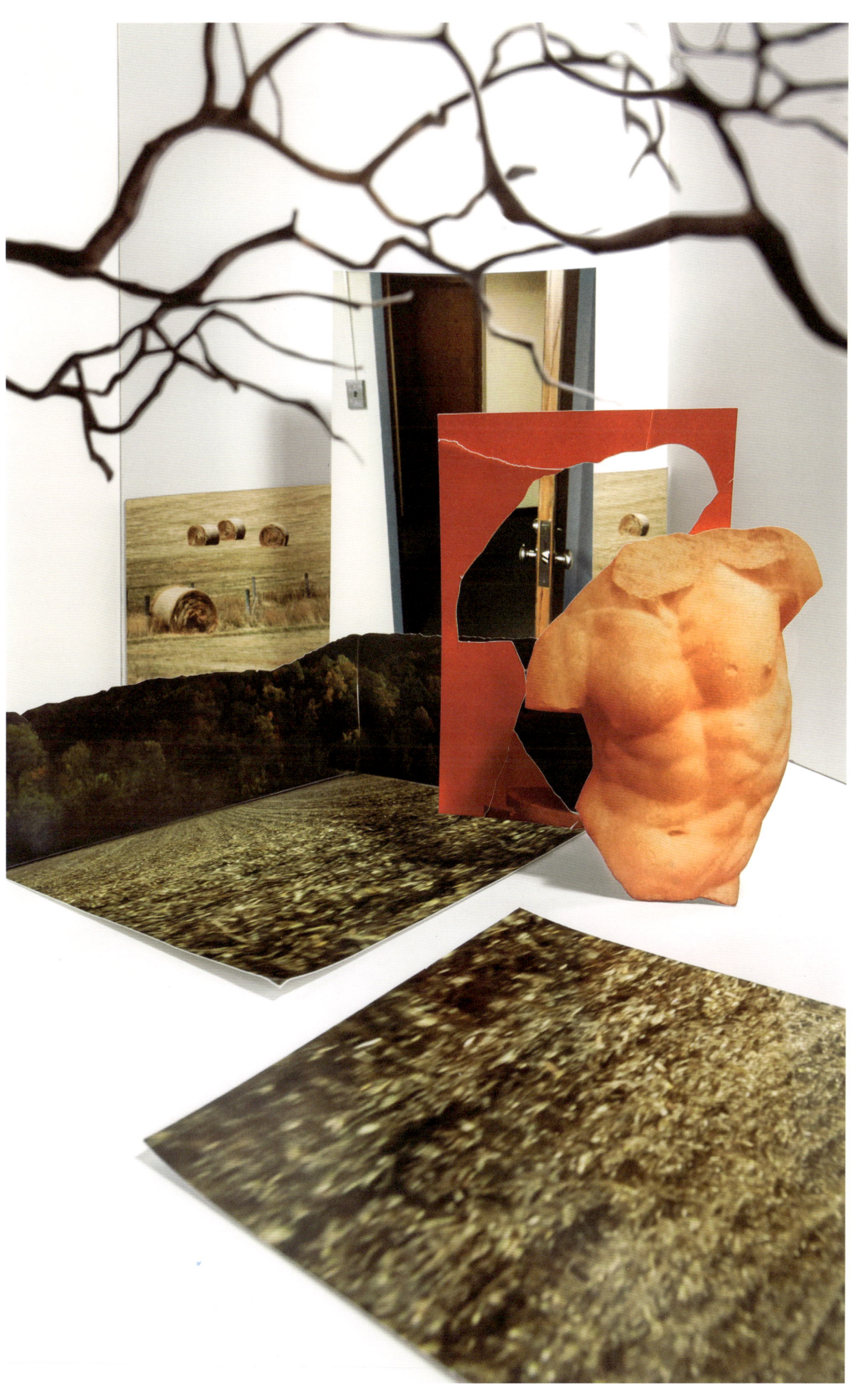

Brandon was from Kansas, which was the most exotic thing an East Coast city girl could imagine. His older brother was stationed in Iraq. Brandon told me that his brother had been one of the soldiers to camp out in Saddam Hussein's palace. I had seen photographs of shirtless Americans swimming in Hussein's pool and I liked feeling close to that. The only other conversation I can pick out from our time together was the night that Brandon stayed up with me until dawn explaining dark matter. I had taken too many drugs and he was the only thing that calmed me.

Brandon showed up at my door with a towel around his waist, having just showered. It had been the same routine for two months. The first time that I'd seen him, he'd been in a river with his clothes draped over the branches of an oak tree. He looked like Huck Finn and I couldn't believe how lucky I was the first time he kissed me. That day, though, I was studying for a French exam and, when I opened my door, his beauty just pissed me off.

This, I said, gesturing to his body. *This isn't gonna happen anymore.*

I closed the door before he could say anything.

~~Daniel~~
~~Mason~~
~~Hudson~~
~~Spencer~~
~~Conor~~
~~Henry~~
~~Brandon~~

Pascal

Pascal was still in high school, but he was French, which seemed to make him older. I lived with his family for a summer while studying at a nearby language institute. I tried not to stare at him during breakfast. For a week, I could barely lift my head.

I was friends with a woman who had been Miss Teen Nepal and loved drinking Long Island iced teas in basement dance clubs. Every night, walking home, I told Miss Teen Nepal that if Pascal was awake when I got home, I would kiss him. He was never awake.

Pascal and I went to museums together, but saw no art. Instead, we circled each other, miscommunicating about the time, lunch plans, which wing to visit next. The morning that I left, I woke him up, early. I had never been in his room before—terrified that his mother would catch me. He opened his door in boxers, half asleep and then walked back toward his bed. I went and sat with him, stared at a poster of a pop singer on his wall, felt self-conscious. There's no nuance or subtlety to be had in a second language, spoken as poorly as I spoke it, so I kissed him and said no when he asked if he should write to me. He shrugged and went back to sleep.

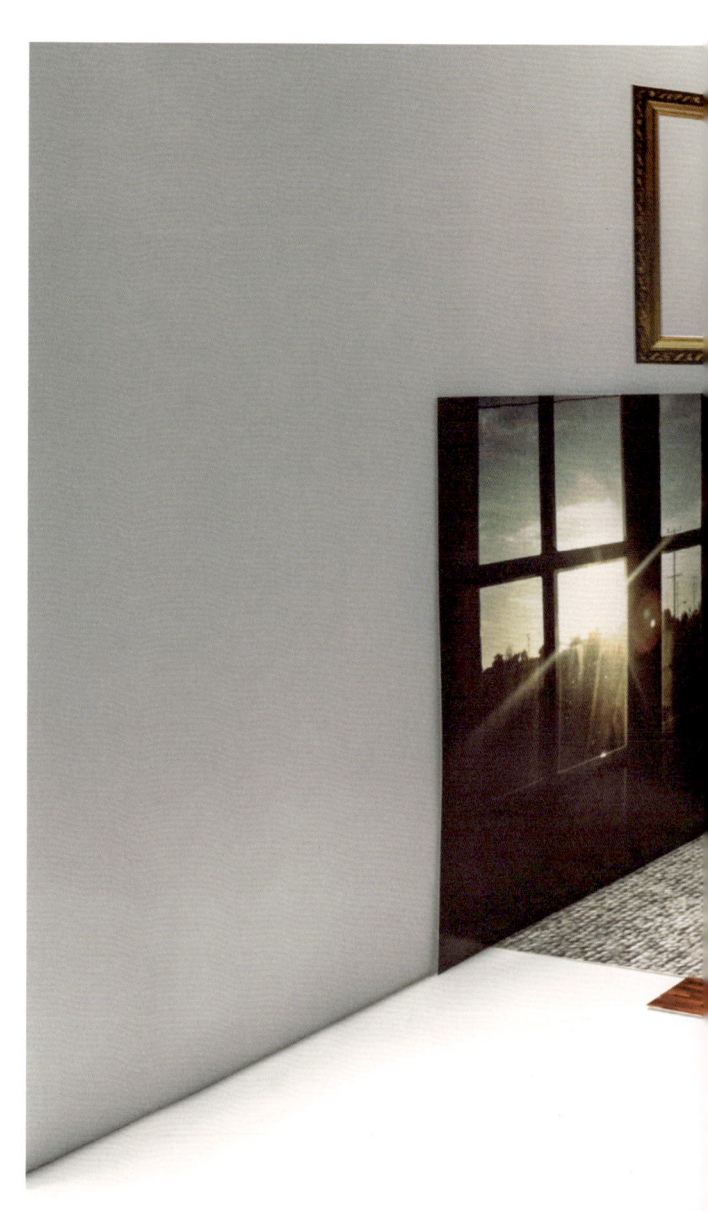

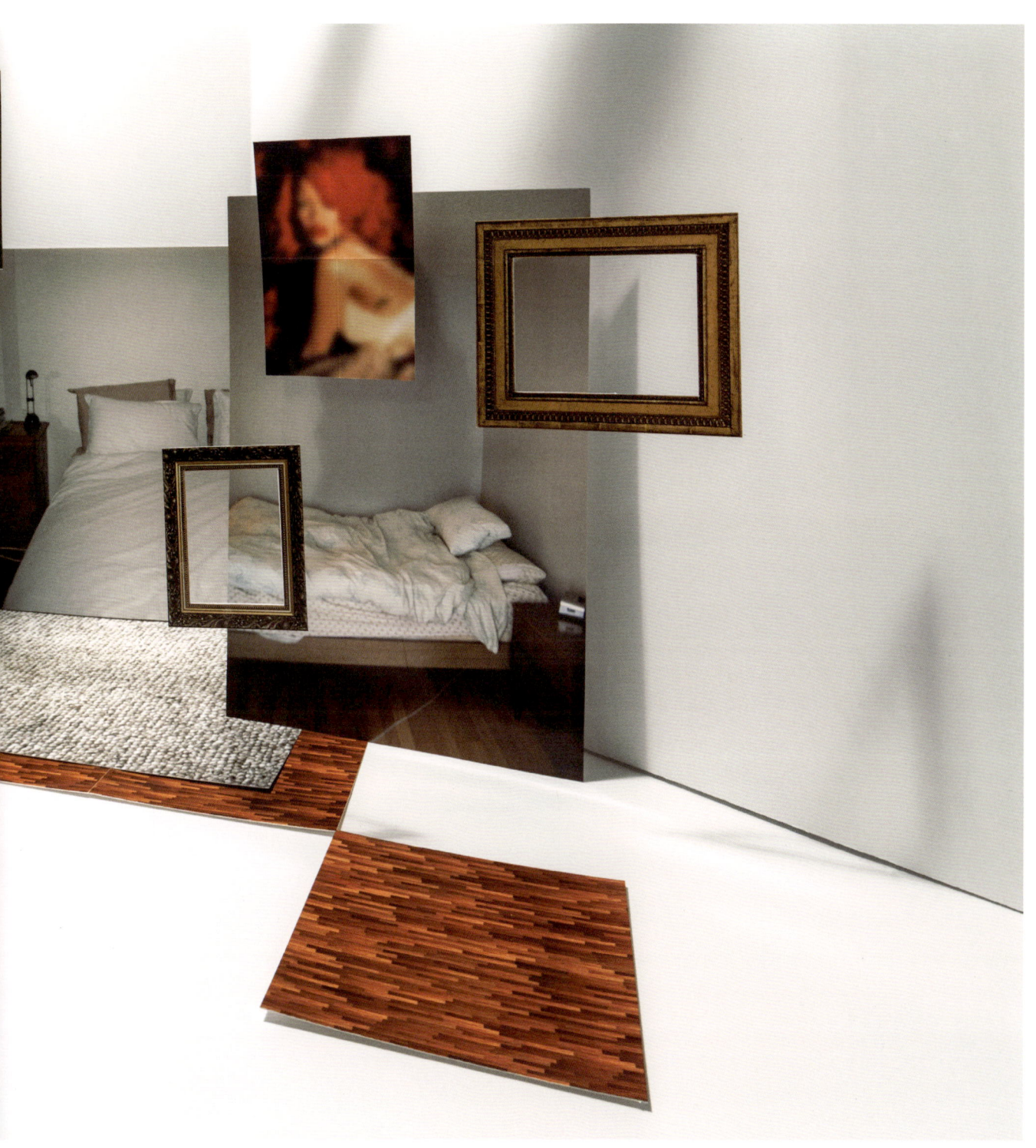

~~Daniel~~
~~Mason~~
~~Hudson~~
~~Spencer~~
~~Conor~~
~~Henry~~
~~Brandon~~
~~Pascal~~

Ray

Ray lived in the type of town that presidents retire to. I took a train in, over a holiday weekend. While I waited for him to pick me up in his parents' car, I looked around the station with all its dark wood and parked luxury sedans. It wasn't the type of place that I'd expected him to be from. At the house, his mother showed me where to put my things, in the guest bedroom. She was uncomfortable, but not unfriendly.

We went to the movies. His little sisters wanted to come but Ray said, *No.* During the movie, my eye started to itch. By the time we were back at the house, I had full-blown pink eye. His mom was sweet about it, but I could tell she was annoyed that I'd brought a disease into her home. If we could just stay together long enough, it would become one of those half-forgotten things you laugh about, but falling asleep that night, I knew that we'd never make it. I was destined to be known as *that girlfriend with pink eye* and it would never be funny.

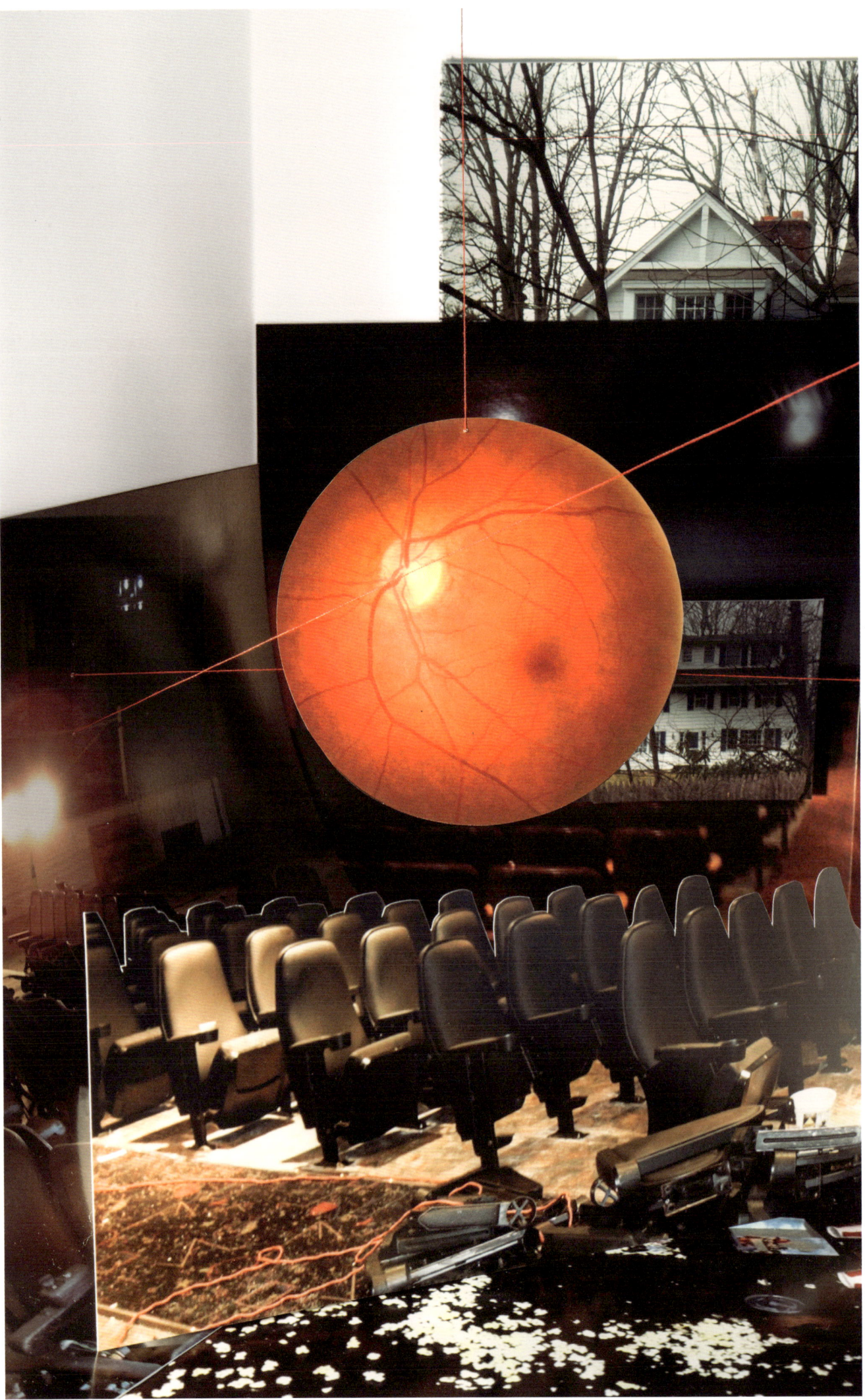

~~Daniel~~
~~Mason~~
~~Hudson~~
~~Spencer~~
~~Conor~~
~~Henry~~
~~Brandon~~
~~Pascal~~
~~Ray~~

Jimmy

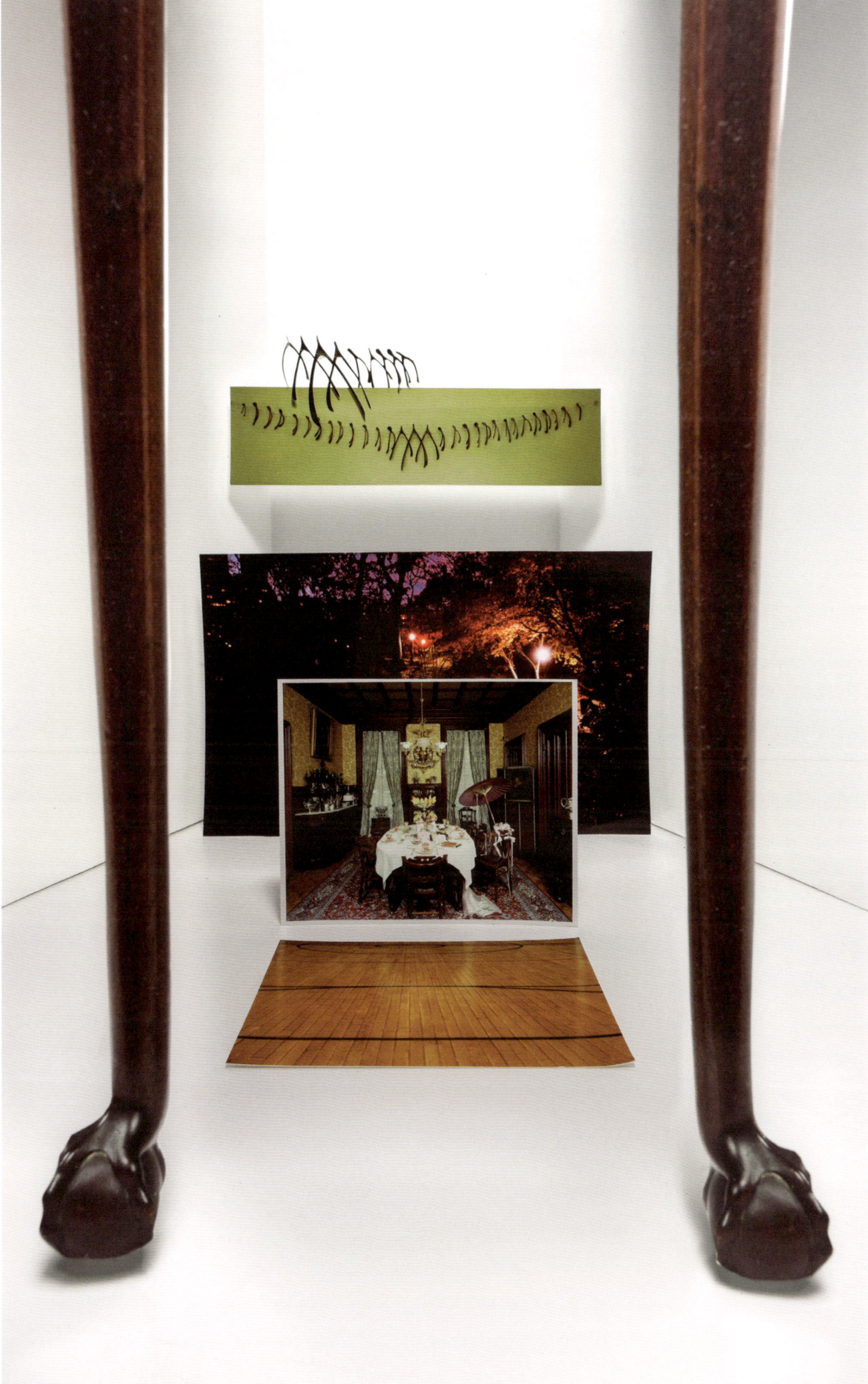

As children, Jimmy and I spent our time under the dining table. His mother would roast a chicken every Sunday. If we were good listeners, she would give us the wishbone and tell us to pull. Even then, in purple leggings and dusty hair, I wished for Jimmy. Every single time that I wrapped my small fingers around the bone, I said a quick prayer for the larger piece, believing that I could secure our happiness. For years, Jimmy got every candle, bone, lucky eyelash—every hope for my future was in that lanky body of his.

It had been a decade since running into Jimmy in a coat closet at a friend's bat-mitzvah, but I still thought about him. I found him online. It only took a few minutes, even drunk. We made plans for that weekend.

From our first exchanges, it was like I could feel my heart breaking—not my heart exactly, but a smaller, simpler version of it. It was as though my chest had Russian nesting dolls in it—containing every stage of love that I'd known. I felt the tiniest ones cracking as Jimmy told me that he was a gym teacher. *Crack.* He smoked menthol cigarettes. *Crack.* He asked me if the art house film playing in the bar was a *porno*. *CRACK.*

I drank a lot that night and kissed him anyway. We bought a flask on the corner and walked along the park, passing it back and forth. *I loved you*, I told him, with a big smile, because it wasn't even sad anymore. It was already hilarious, how wrong I'd been.

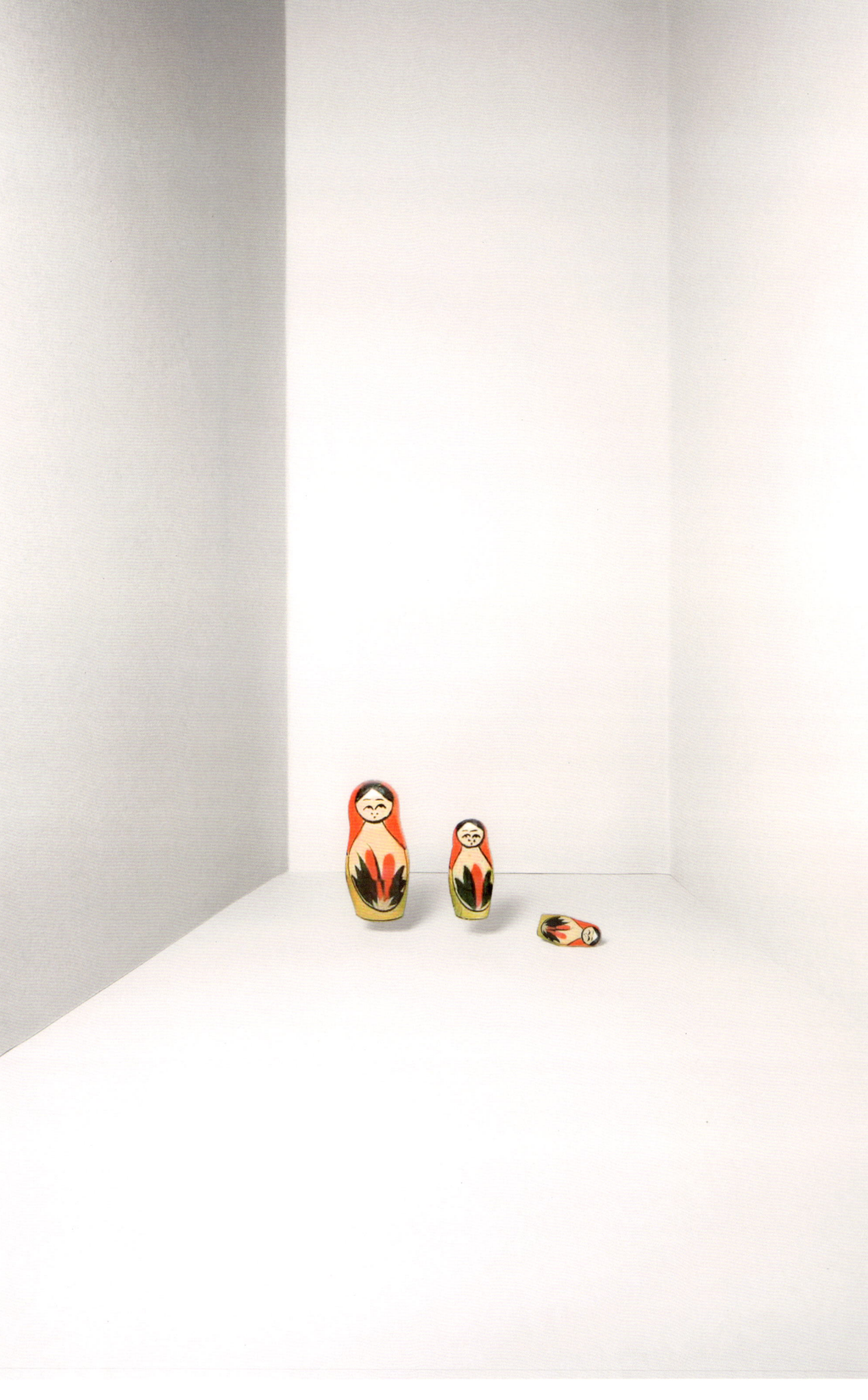

~~Daniel~~
~~Mason~~
~~Hudson~~
~~Spencer~~
~~Conor~~
~~Henry~~
~~Brandon~~
~~Pascal~~
~~Ray~~
~~Jimmy~~

Patrick

I moved into my boyfriend's studio apartment just as he was leaving for Europe. I spent a week pretending that he was watching me. I ate cereal in my underwear and read his most impressive books. I stood at the window and smoked a cigarette, conjuring his face. I drank wine and took long baths. I was trying to be the girlfriend he thought I was. By the end of the week I was exhausted and still had two weeks left, alone.

Patrick showed up the second week, with a ladder under his arm. The landlord had sent him to finish some wiring that hadn't been completed before the move-in date. It was early in the afternoon. I was drinking a beer and wasn't wearing a bra. Patrick noticed both things and smiled at me. There was nowhere in the apartment to go, so I sat at the dining table and watched Patrick work. I asked him questions about boats and offered him a beer, which he finished in four or five long drinks.

As he took panels off the outlets I could see tangles of wires, hidden from sight. There was more going on than I ever realized and Patrick told me that was always how it was. I got myself another beer while he finished working. Watching as he carefully returned each of the panels to the walls, I fantasized about having sex with him.

Before I could think of what to say or do, he was folding up his ladder and pocketing his screwdriver. He left and I kept drinking. From then on, it was Patrick I pictured when I imagined someone watching me.

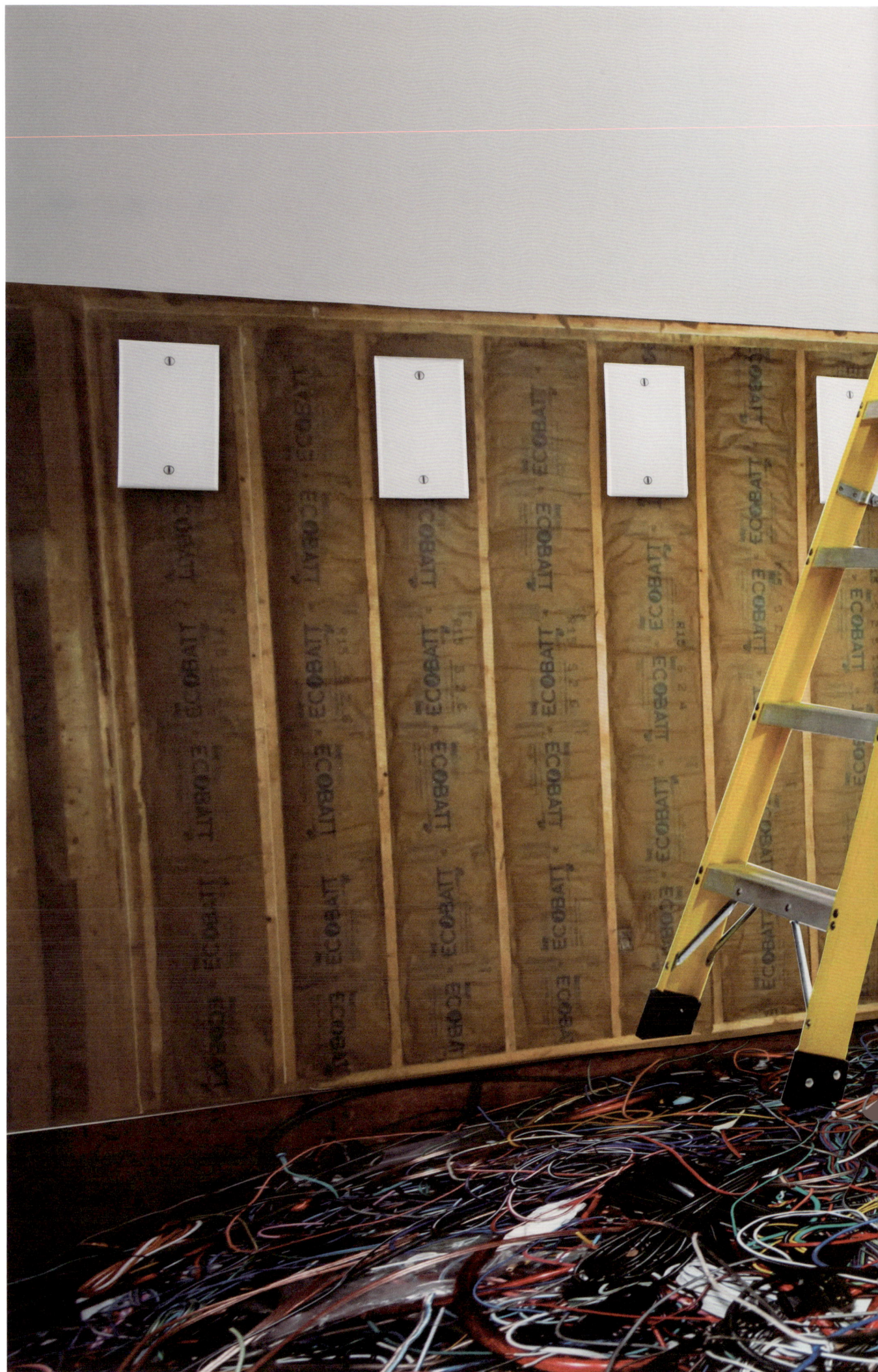

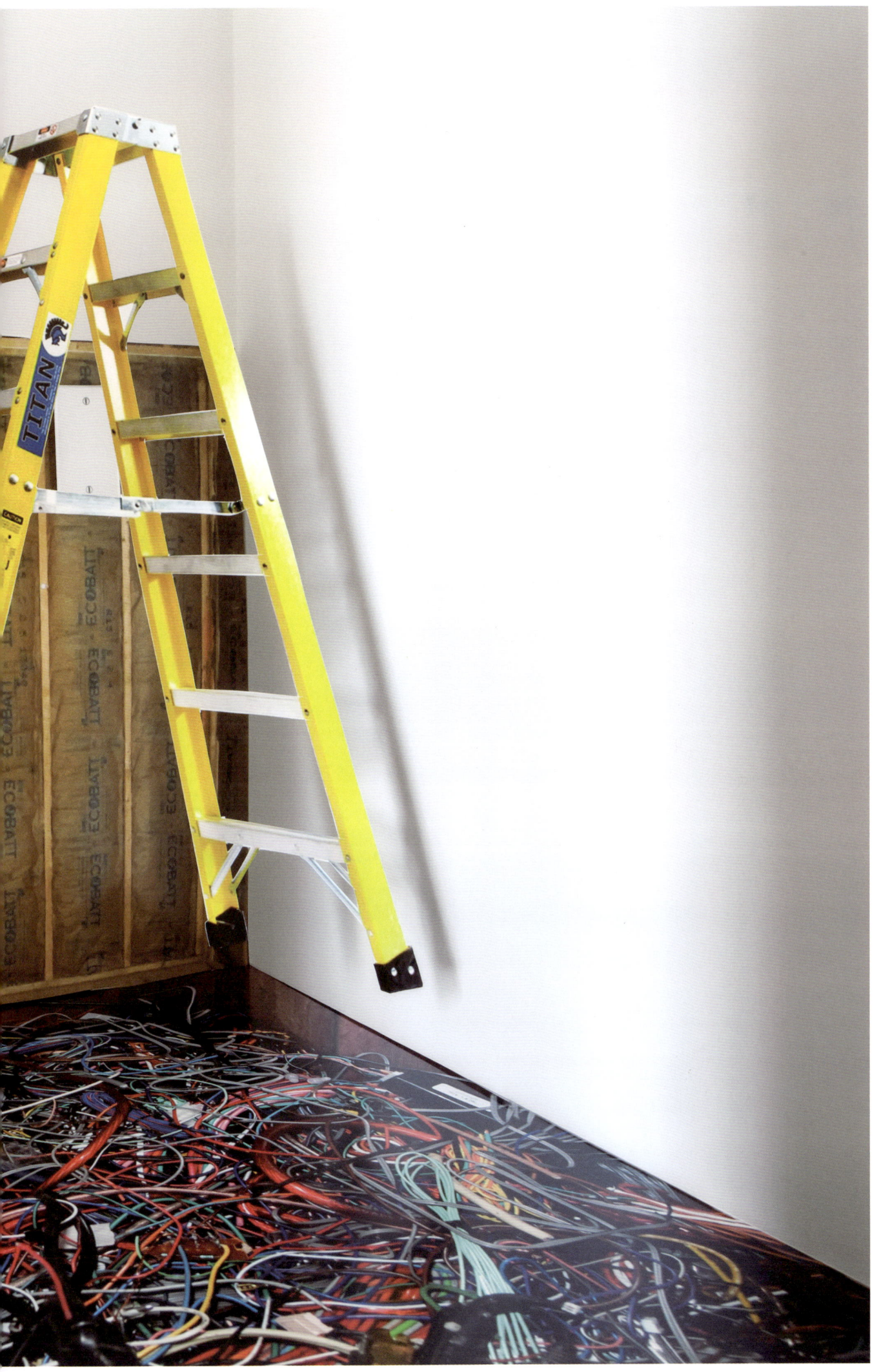

~~Daniel~~
~~Mason~~
~~Hudson~~
~~Spencer~~
~~Conor~~
~~Henry~~
~~Brandon~~
~~Pascal~~
~~Ray~~
~~Jimmy~~
~~Patrick~~

Kyle

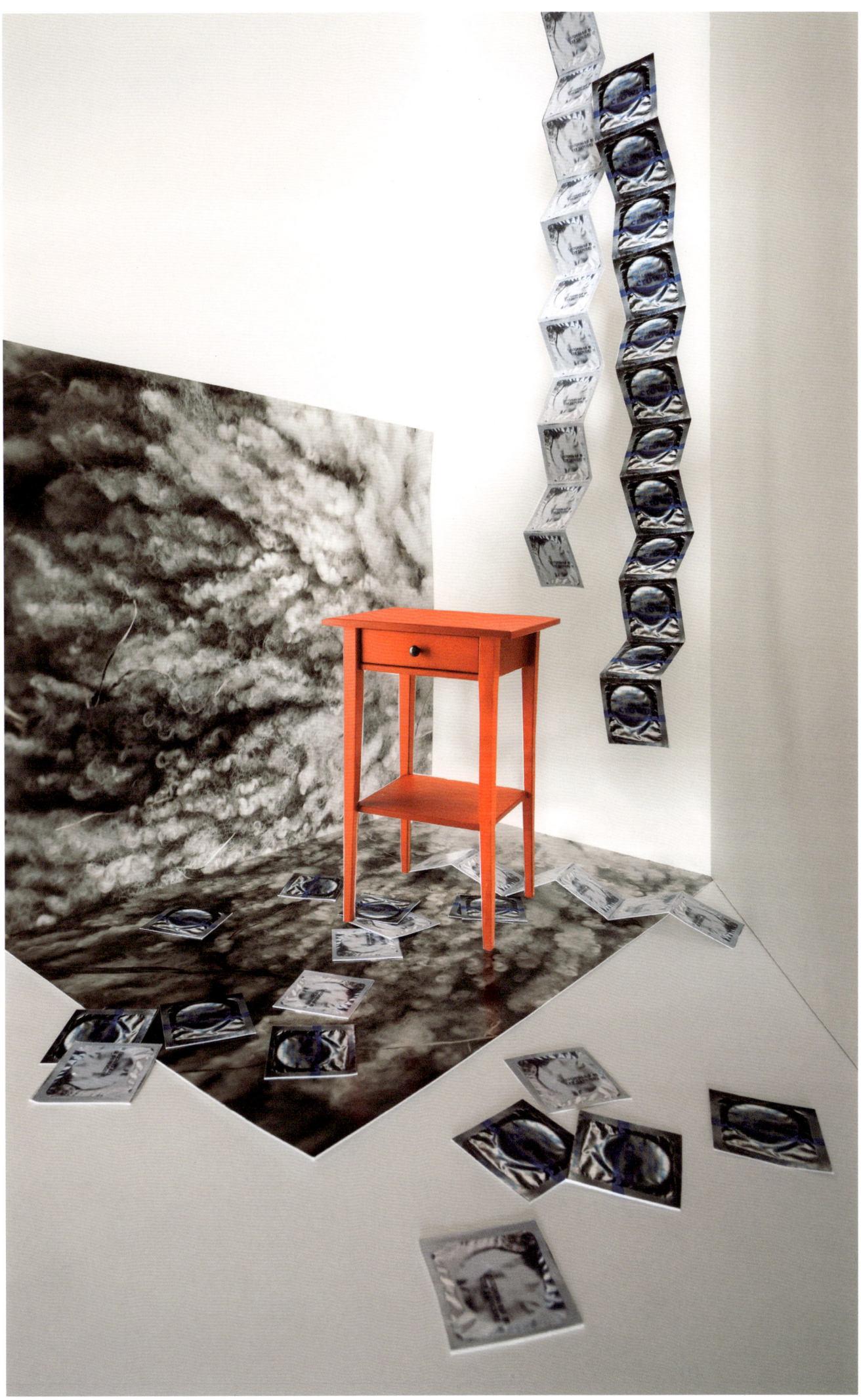

Kyle ordered condoms online, by the hundred. It played as bravado, but stemmed from shame. Once, I'd asked him to pick me up a box of tampons at the grocery store and he'd refused, flat-out. When his mother came to visit, he swept all my things into a basket and hid it under the sink.

Kyle kept his condoms in his nightstand, on his side of the bed. His side of the bed was the one by the door because, even though Kyle was terrified of touching a tampon, he would have shown no hesitation at protecting me if anyone had ever burst through the front door. I loved that.

When we'd started dating, he'd ordered a new box, even though he probably had thirty left from his last relationship. I felt optimistic as I watched him dump one hundred silver packages into the nightstand. I liked the way that they'd folded like Jacob's ladders.

That summer unrolled like a thick, wool blanket. No storms, no power outages, no fights. Nothing. It was late August when I saw him open the drawer and realized that there were only six condoms left inside. I asked if he'd ordered more and he said that he hadn't remembered to. I tried to rouse myself to feel something, but I just said, *Oh.*

~~Daniel~~
~~Mason~~
~~Hudson~~
~~Spencer~~
~~Conor~~
~~Henry~~
~~Brandon~~
~~Pascal~~
~~Ray~~
~~Jimmy~~
~~Patrick~~
~~Kyle~~

Lee

I had just had my tonsils out. The pills had made me sick and skinny and everyone liked it. My boyfriend was throwing me an extravagant going-away party in the apartment that we'd shared that summer. The building had been a schoolhouse once, which he thought was very cool. The glass in the windows was old and stood loosely in the panes. It rattled violently in the wind, threatening to break over our heads. Hundreds of insects had died on our windowsills and no one had been able to answer me when I asked why.

The music was loud and fun, but I didn't like the way my boyfriend danced. I'd wondered what our wedding would be like—can a bride refuse to dance with her groom? Late into the night, he found a more willing partner and I found Lee in the hallway, alone. I got him into a dark corner with me. We pressed ourselves into the dusty walls and something about the space that we took up with our bodies convinced me that I could say anything. I confessed that I still listened to the song that he'd recorded for me, the year before, after a long week of alternating finals and acid. Lee just shrugged because we both knew how it had all played out.

The bugs are drawn to the light, he said. *They're trying to get outside. They probably died there, waiting.*

I knew that he was trying to change the subject. I knew that, at best, he didn't love me anymore and, at worst, I was an idiot for thinking that he ever had.

I chose the wrong one, I said in a flat voice. *I just need you to know that I've realized that.*

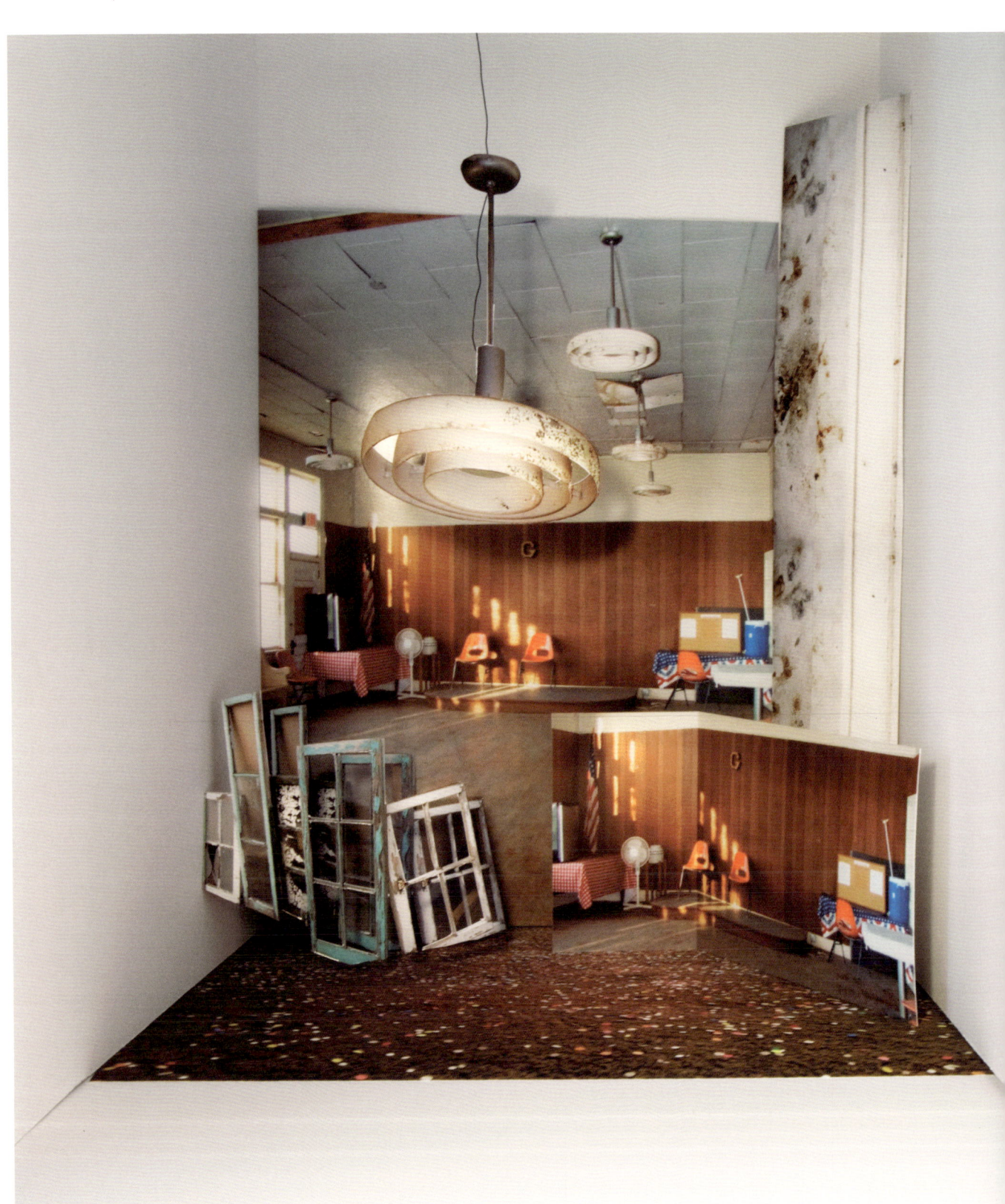

~~Daniel~~
~~Mason~~
~~Hudson~~
~~Spencer~~
~~Conor~~
~~Henry~~
~~Brandon~~
~~Pascal~~
~~Ray~~
~~Jimmy~~
~~Patrick~~
~~Kyle~~
~~Lee~~

Naomi

~~Daniel~~
~~Mason~~
~~Hudson~~
~~Spencer~~
~~Conor~~

Naomi and I hadn't seen much of each other since high school. Pure coincidence landed us in the same study-abroad program during our junior year of college. We were living in Paris. We drank a lot. We saw each other almost every day. We were in a bar that looked like a cave and it was so cold outside that I never wanted to leave. My boyfriend was coming to visit me for New Year's Eve. Naomi was drinking alcohol that tasted like licorice and asking me questions about fucking men. Naomi thought straight people were fascinating—like a small species of insects that she'd discovered in the Amazon. I told her that if we got him drunk enough, maybe she could watch. *Straight people always fuck on New Year's Eve.* I said it as though I were a cultural diplomat.

Naomi was renting a tiny apartment in a building of old ladies. In the elevator, she said *SHHH* so loudly that I thought she'd wake them all. I undressed while she was getting me water. I kissed her, which I'd done before, but this was more earnest. My boyfriend was coming in one week. It was the holidays. I'd barely understood anything that anyone had said to me for five months.

You're straight, she said.

You always fuck straight girls.

You have a boyfriend, she said.

This is different.

Just because I'm a woman, doesn't mean it's not cheating. She said it like she was talking to a selfish little child.

I woke up the next morning, right there in her bed, still naked. *Well that's something you can't do with a man*, I said.

Nothing happened, she said, *handing me my glass of water.*

That's what I mean, I said.

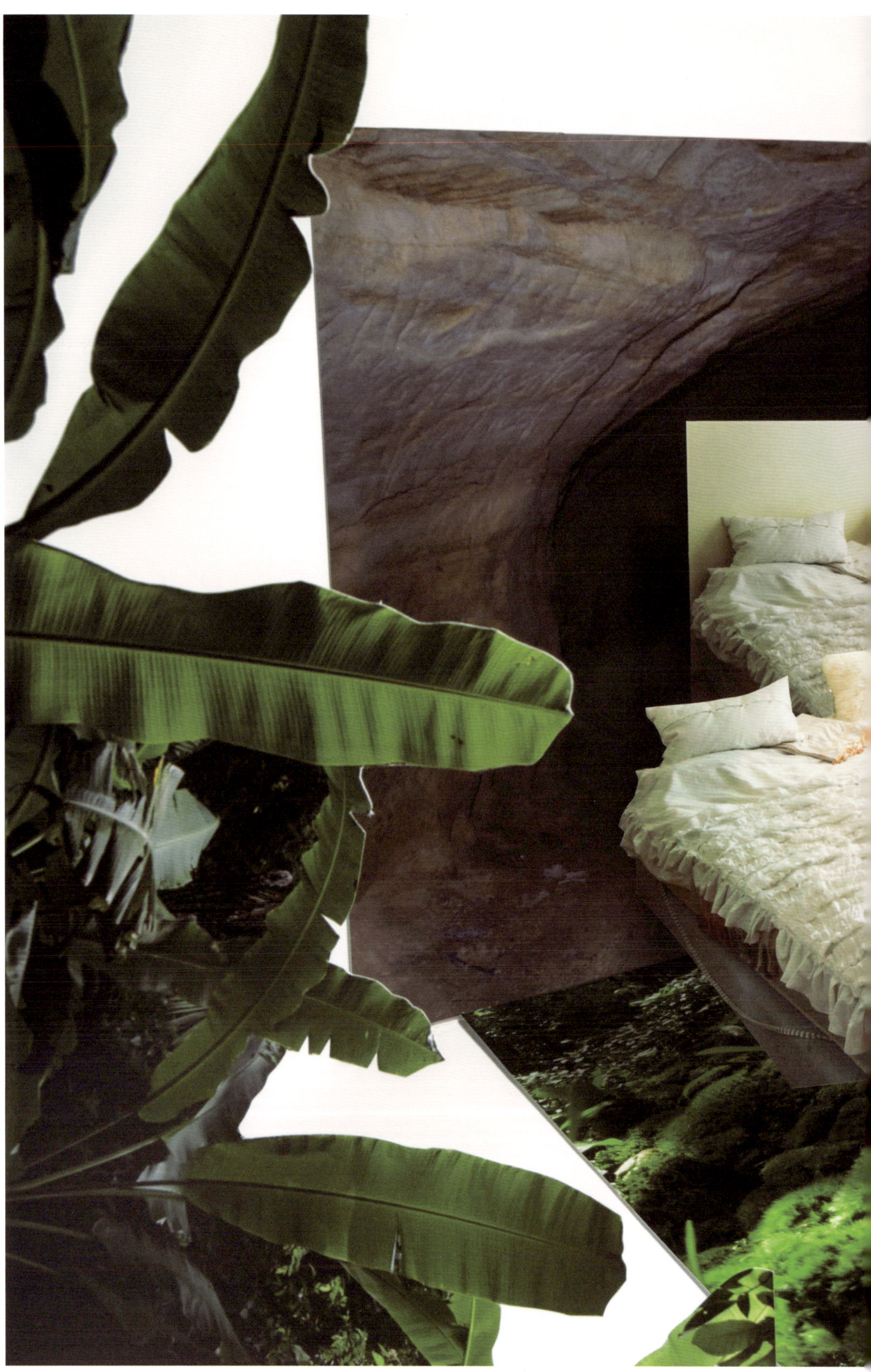

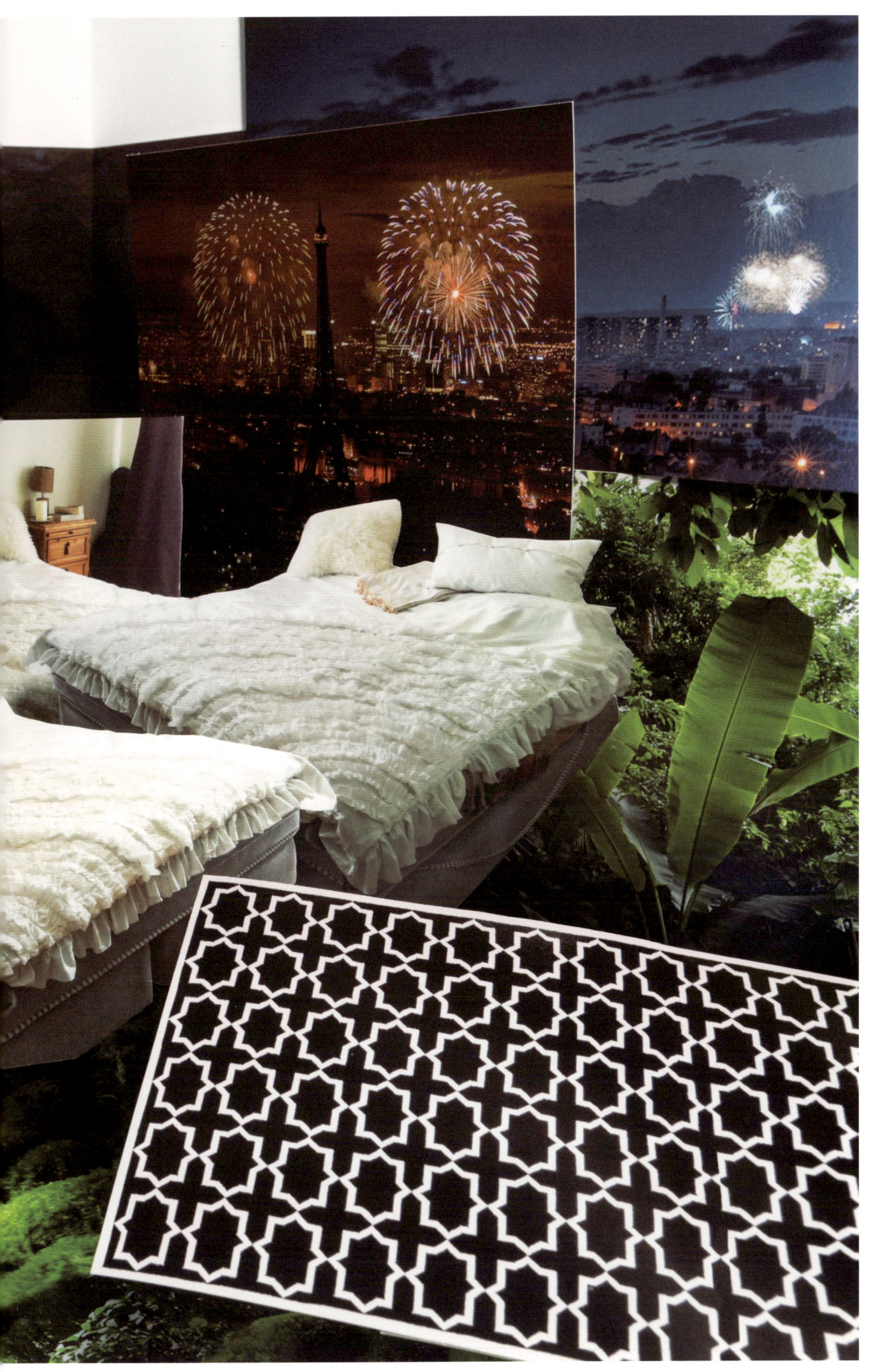

~~Daniel~~
~~Mason~~
~~Hudson~~
~~Spencer~~
~~Conor~~
~~Henry~~
~~Brandon~~
~~Pascal~~
~~Ray~~
~~Jimmy~~
Patrick
Kyle
~~Lee~~
Naomi

Kyle, again

Kyle and I sat on the edge of the bed while I waited for a friend to come pick me up. He could have driven me himself, but hadn't offered. I told him that I thought he was making a mistake and he said, *Maybe*.

He was breaking up with me the way you'd break up with a girl in middle school. We were older. We lived together. I tried to read between the lines, knowing that there had to be more. Separating all our stuff was a process that demanded more of a reason than the ones that he'd given me. Kyle was, above all else, a coward.

I stared and squinted at him until the truth of it just landed right in my palm—a cold, heavy marble, dropped from above. The evidence that came together in that moment had been spread out over months and, later, would feel impossible to neglect. But I hadn't seen it. He was cheating on me. It was sharp and clear—all in one second. She was a friend of mine, dating a friend of his. He was probably in love with her. She didn't make him wear condoms. It all came to me so quickly.

Do you know how many times I didn't cheat on you? was all that I could come up with to say.

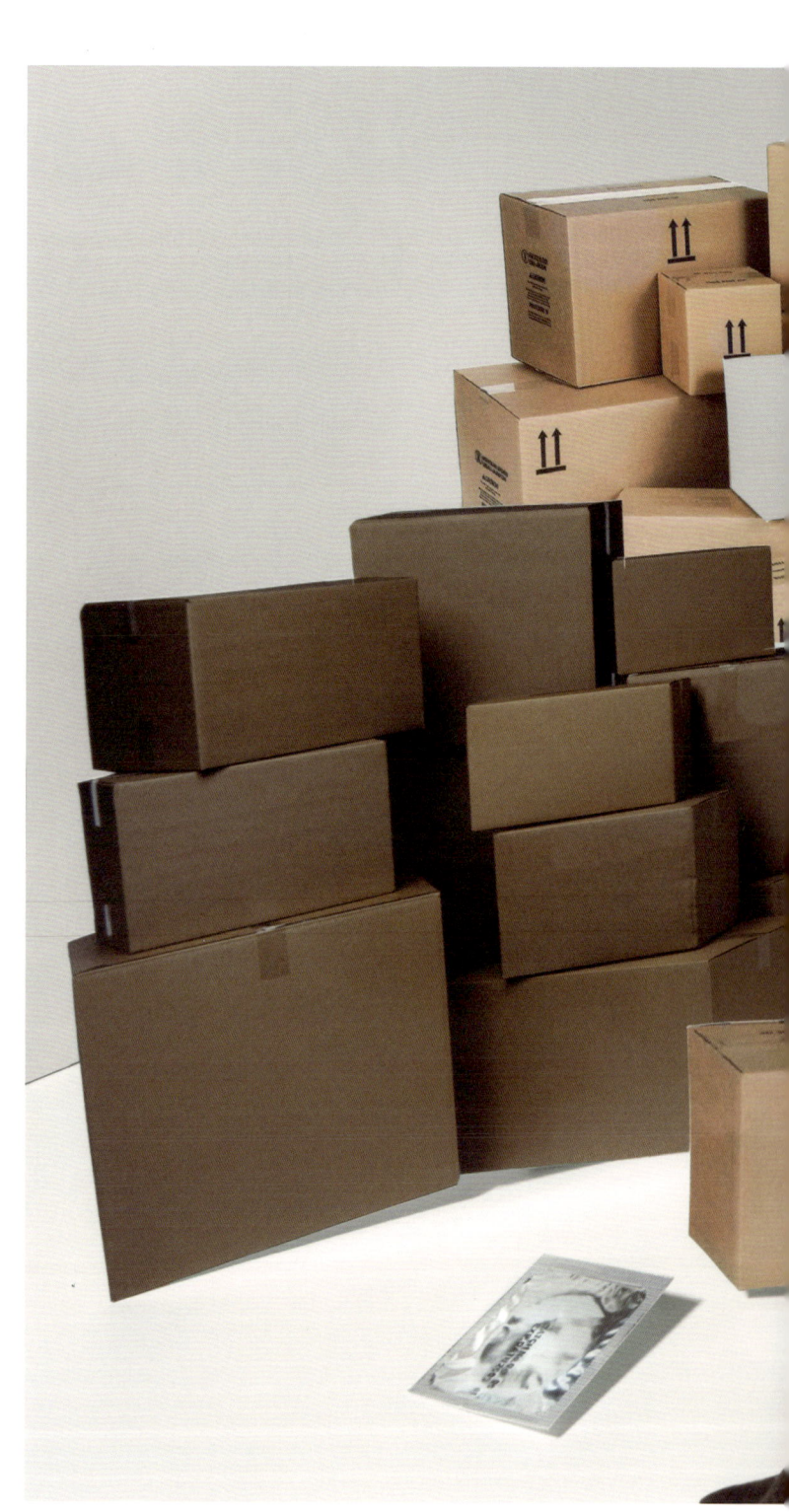

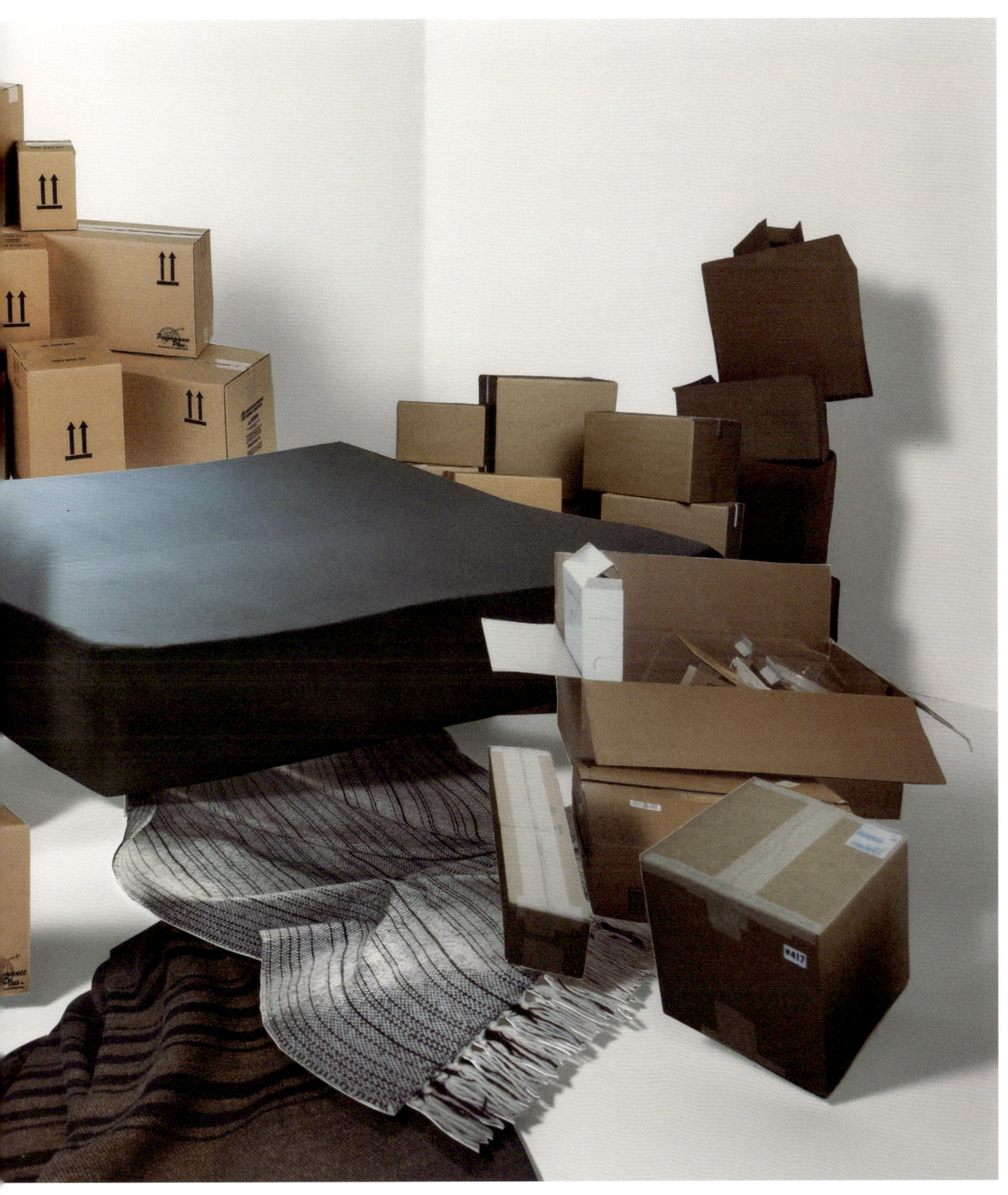

~~Daniel~~
~~Mason~~
~~Hudson~~
~~Spencer~~
~~Conor~~
~~Henry~~
~~Brandon~~
~~Pascal~~
~~Ray~~
~~Jimmy~~
~~Patrick~~
~~Kyle~~
~~Lee~~
~~Naomi~~
~~Kyle, again~~

Sam

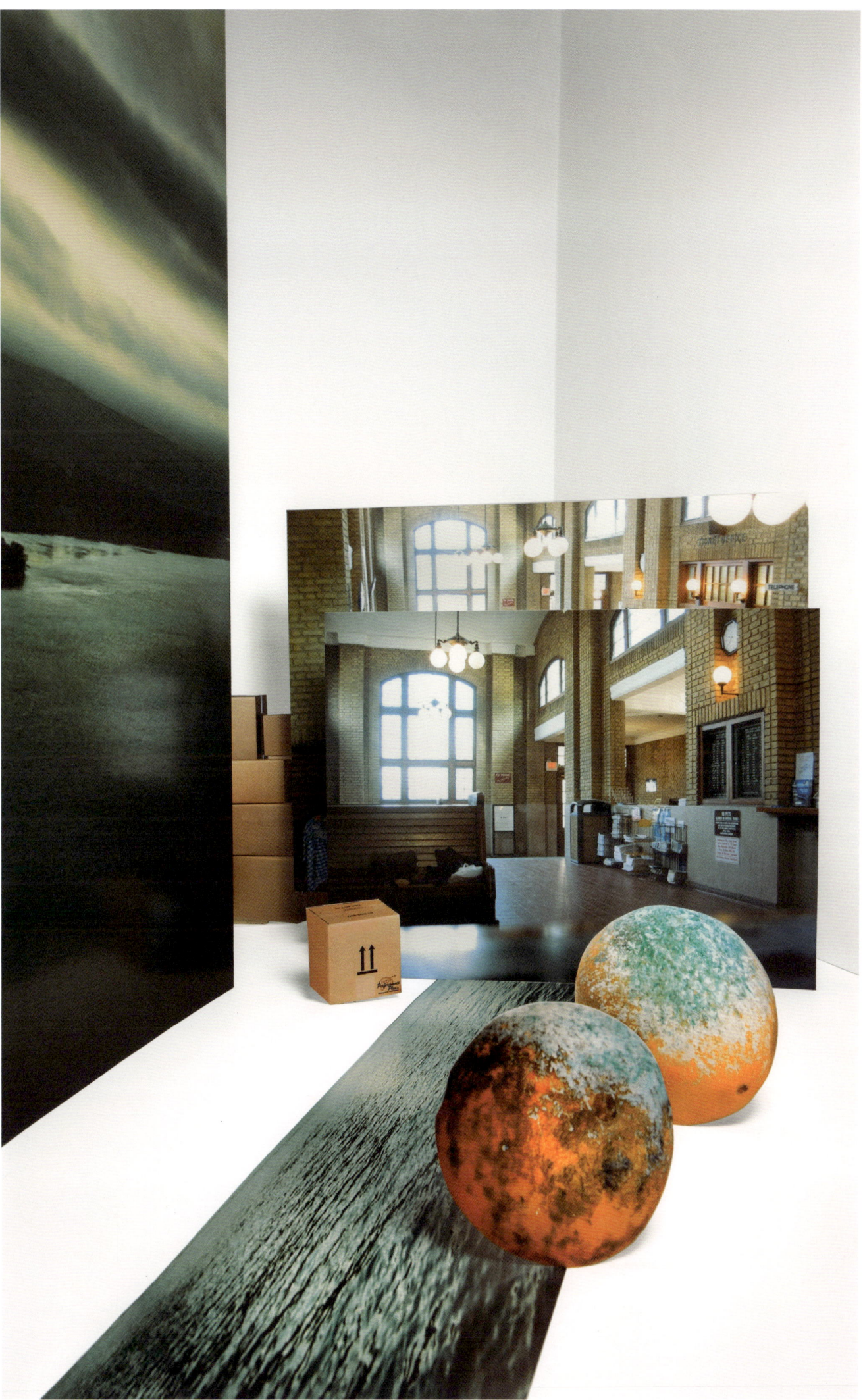

Being with Sam was marked by a constant hum of his need for approval. He deserved better, but I was angry those months. Our exes had cheated on us with each other. It wasn't Sam's fault, but I punished him for it anyway. I didn't want to admit that I liked his jokes or the way he gave head or his beard. I just wanted to be mean.

I once caught myself wondering if his mother would like me. I wavered constantly, though. I ignored his phone calls, kicked him out in the middle of the night, refused to laugh when he needed me to. I left town for the weekend and didn't tell him where I was going.

I hadn't expected to miss him. I called him from the train and told him that I was heading home. Without having to ask, I heard him pick up his keys. I stared at the Hudson River and tried to pry myself open. I wanted to tell Sam that I'd missed him. I wanted to tell him that we should both stop sleeping with other people.

We weren't even halfway to town by the time all of my affirmations from the train had slipped away. I resented him again, for nothing. I wondered why he hadn't had anything better to do than come pick me up. I was as rotten as every piece of fruit in his kitchen.

Van Morrison came on the radio and I could feel him anticipating the lyrics—*I want to rock your gypsy soul.* Sam went to turn the volume up and I imagined him believing, in his midwestern way, that I would hear those lyrics and know that he was speaking to me. I hit his hand away before he reached the knob.

Just don't, was all I said.

~~Daniel~~
~~Mason~~
~~Hudson~~
~~Spencer~~
~~Conor~~
~~Henry~~
~~Brandon~~
~~Pascal~~
~~Ray~~
~~Jimmy~~
~~Patrick~~
~~Kyle~~
~~Lee~~
~~Naomi~~
~~Kyle, again~~
~~Sam~~

Jack

Jack and I were friends. We were attracted. I wanted someone to say goodnight to and he wanted someone to go out to breakfast with. We were both hung up on other people and knew that we were standing in for them, but we didn't mind. In some ways, it was the most equitable relationship that I'd known.

He had a photograph of his ex-girlfriend framed on his nightstand. She was standing on a beach, trying to prevent her hat from blowing away. I knew that Jack had been the one holding the camera. Seeing her next to his bed like that didn't hurt me, but it did pierce something. The comfort of our bubble deflated slowly. I spent too much time wondering about where that beach was and who had bought the metal picture frame and which of them had put her inside it.

Despite never having wanted more from him, I began to feel neglected. My feelings for him weren't deep, but I felt bitter that his were similarly shallow. We remained friends. Quickly, it was as though nothing had happened at all, because it barely had.

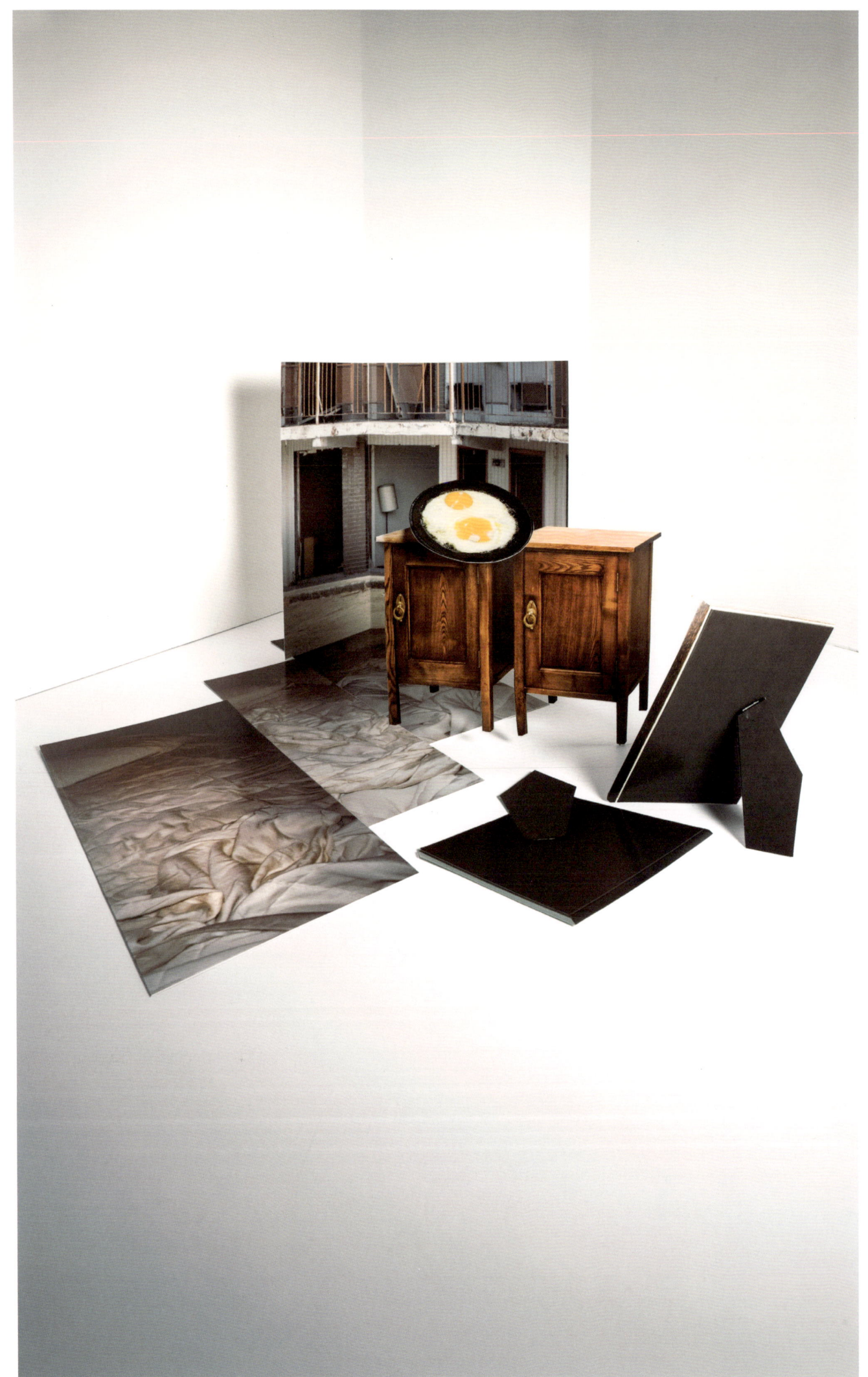

~~Daniel~~
~~Mason~~
~~Hudson~~
~~Spencer~~
~~Conor~~
~~Henry~~
~~Brandon~~
~~Pascal~~
~~Ray~~
~~Jimmy~~
~~Patrick~~
~~Kyle~~
~~Lee~~
~~Naomi~~
~~Kyle, again~~
~~Sam~~
~~Jack~~

Tony

As a teenager, Tony and his friends would pick the locks to vacation homes and raid their liquor cabinets. He lost his virginity in one of those houses. As an adult, Tony was a locksmith. He didn't understand how funny this was. I had thought we were just friends, but I found out that Tony deleted my phone number every Sunday and then had to ask someone for it again every Friday. He didn't want his wife seeing my name in his phone. My roommates told me not to be a homewrecker. I said that it wasn't homewrecking if they were getting divorced anyway.

The more my friends warned me off Tony, the more I wanted to be with him. The idea that I was enough to threaten someone's marriage made me feel like a woman. The possibility of my name in someone's phone having enough power to dismantle a relationship fascinated me.

Tony left his wife that spring. He started calling on Tuesdays, asking me to get drunk with him. I stopped answering.

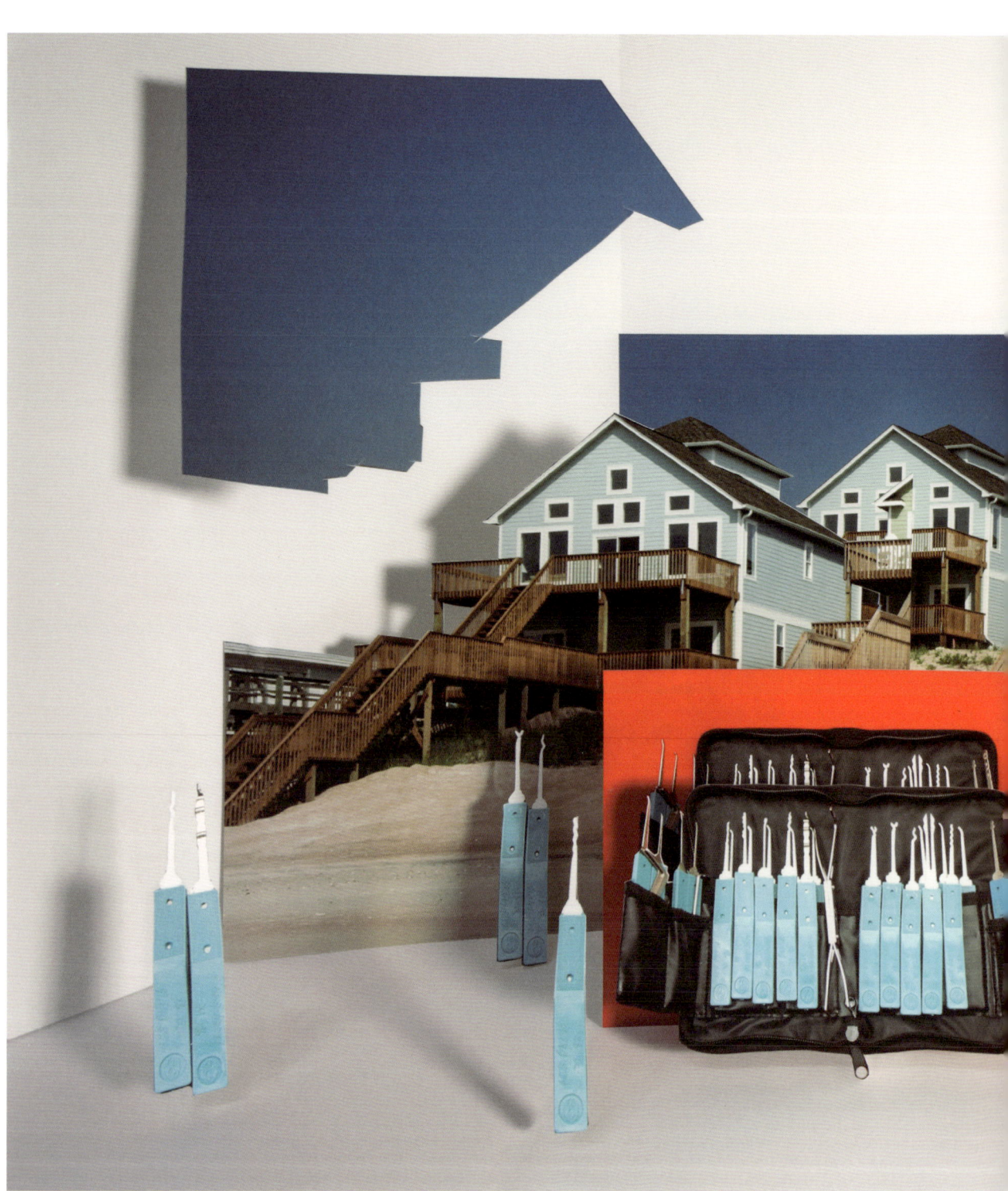

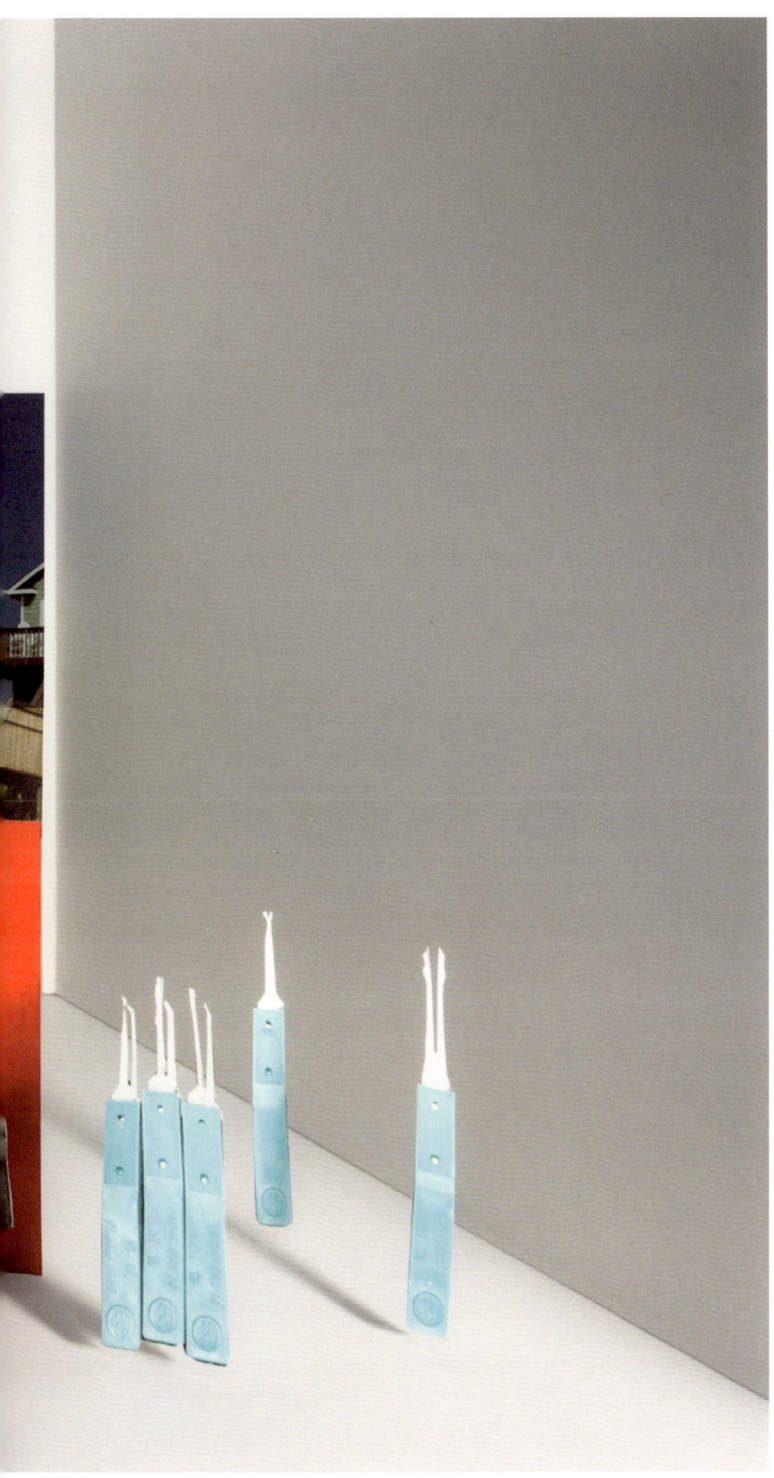

~~Daniel~~
~~Mason~~
~~Hudson~~
~~Spencer~~
~~Conor~~
Henry
Brandon
~~Pascal~~
~~Ray~~
~~Jimmy~~
Patrick
~~Kyle~~
~~Lee~~
~~Naomi~~
~~Kyle, again~~
~~Sam~~
~~Jack~~
~~Tony~~

Greg

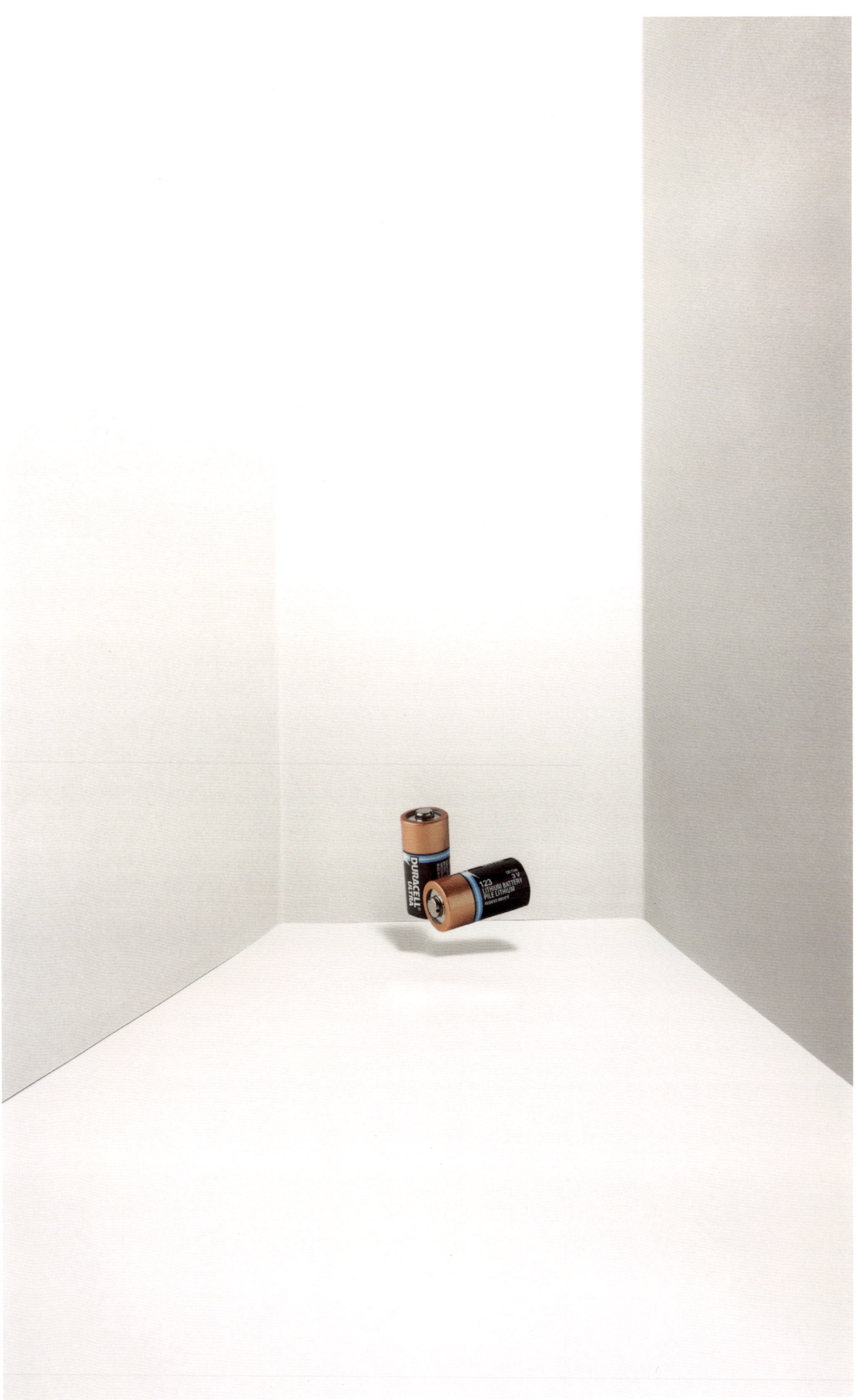

Greg was too old for me and we both knew it. Our relationship was innocent, but no one believes that when the guy is twice your age. My friends didn't like me spending so much time with a townie and his friends thought I was trouble. We'd walk into a bar together and the woman working behind the counter would just shake her head. Sometimes we'd try to explain, but we mostly let people think what they would.

Greg told me early on that the ball was in my court. He explained that it wouldn't be right if he was the one to make a move. He drove over in an ice storm to make sure that I had beer and batteries. On his way to work, he would stop by my house and plow out my driveway, before I was even awake. It made my housemates look at me funny.

On one of the first warm days, Greg drove me across the river, where nobody would recognize us. He bought me lunch in a small town and, for once, we didn't drink. When he asked if he should take me back home, all I could say was, Not yet. He drove me to a barn silo on a rundown piece of land. There was a door missing and Greg told me to be careful. Inside, there was a seven-foot drop, straight down. When my eyes adjusted, I could see that the floor was covered in animal skeletons—raccoons, foxes, cats. Greg told me that animals fell down there and had no way of getting back up.

I want you to stay, he said, looking straight at me. *I'd build you a house and get you chickens and you'd have a place to do your work. But I think you'd feel trapped.* I didn't say anything but wondered if I'd ever get an offer like that again. Greg shrugged. *I don't want you to think I wouldn't have asked.*

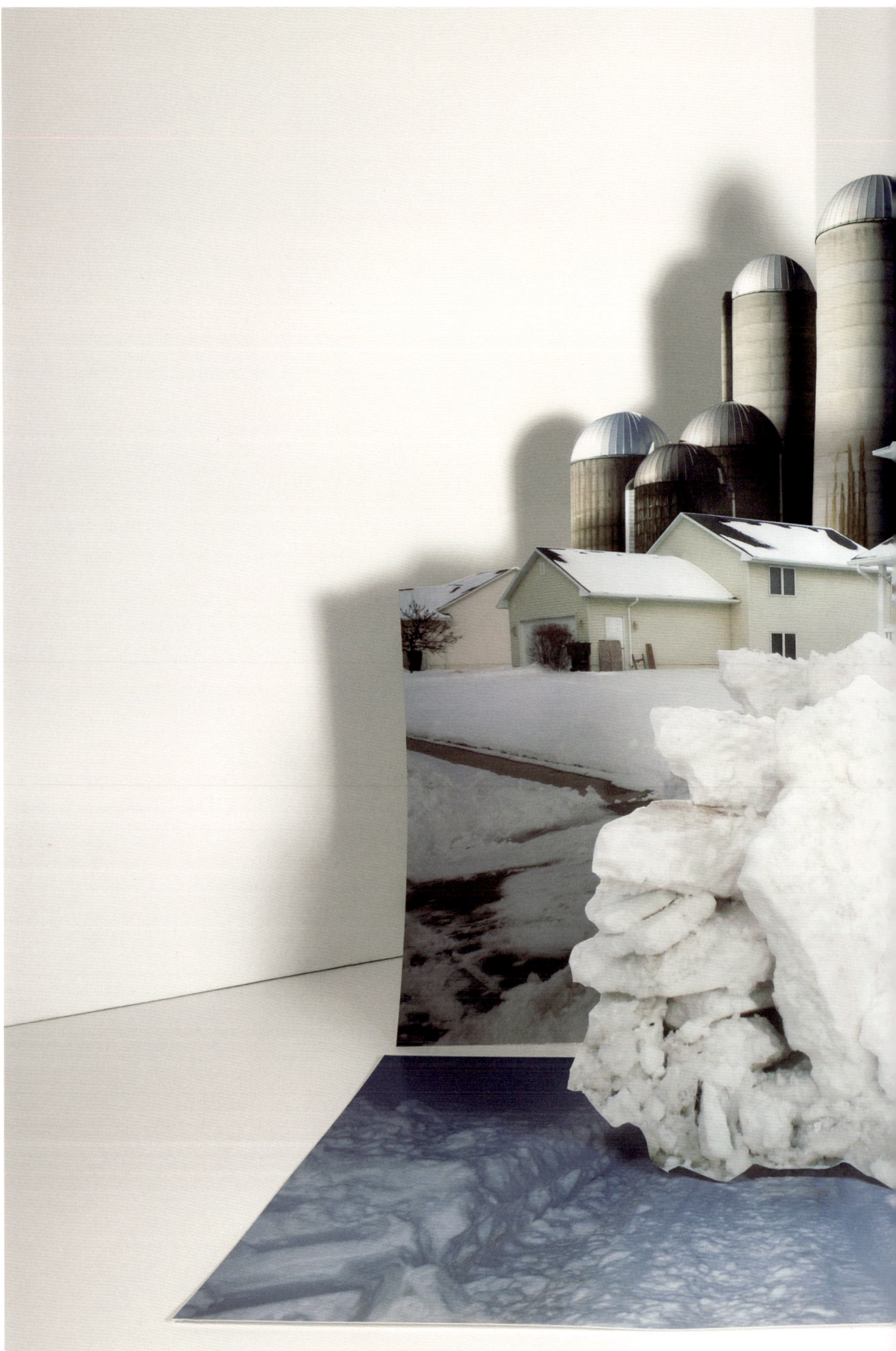

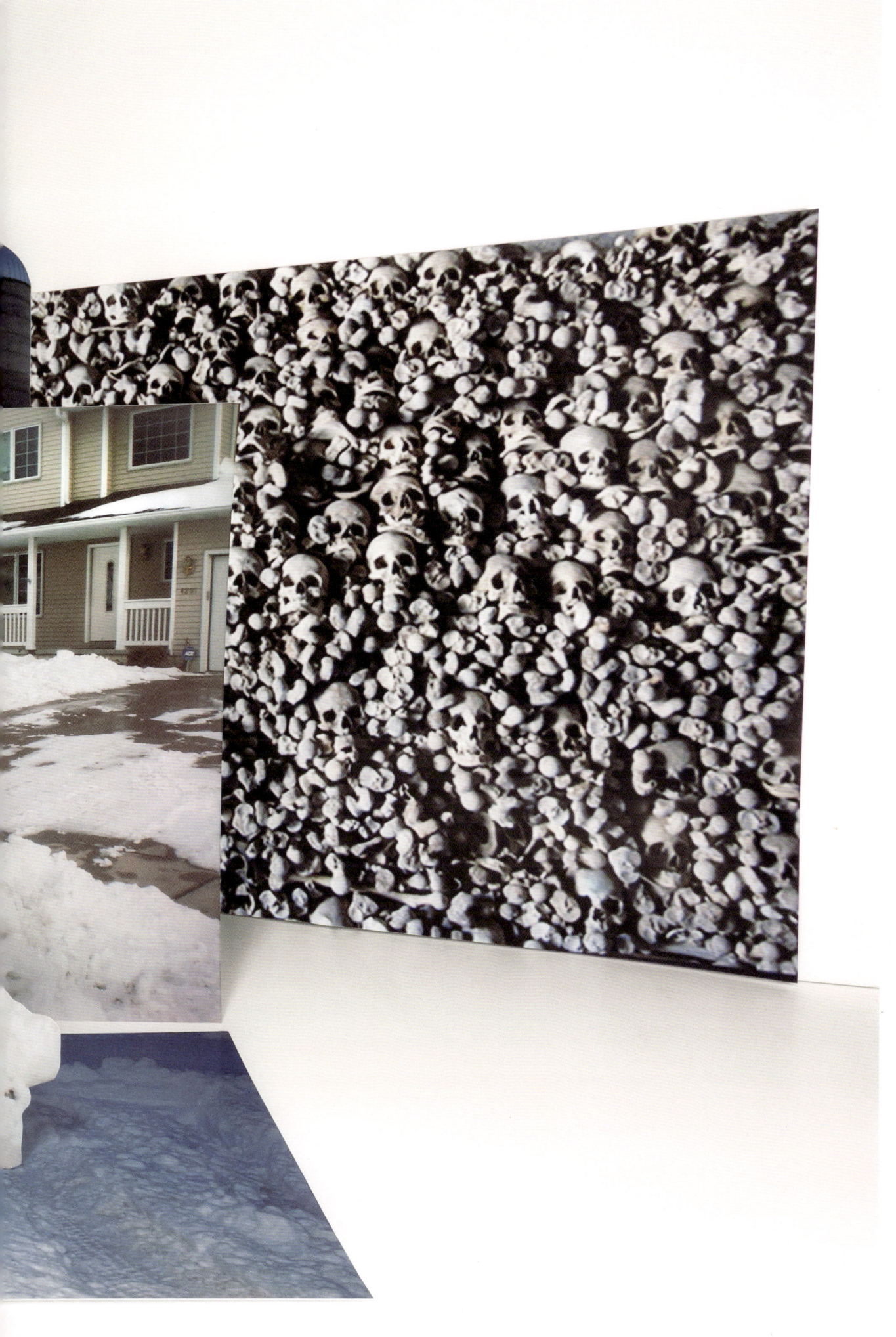

~~Daniel~~
~~Mason~~
Hudson
Spencer
~~Conor~~
Henry
Brandon
~~Pascal~~
~~Ray~~
Jimmy
Patrick
Kyle
~~Lee~~
Naomi
Kyle, again
~~Sam~~
Jack
~~Tony~~
~~Greg~~

Bennett

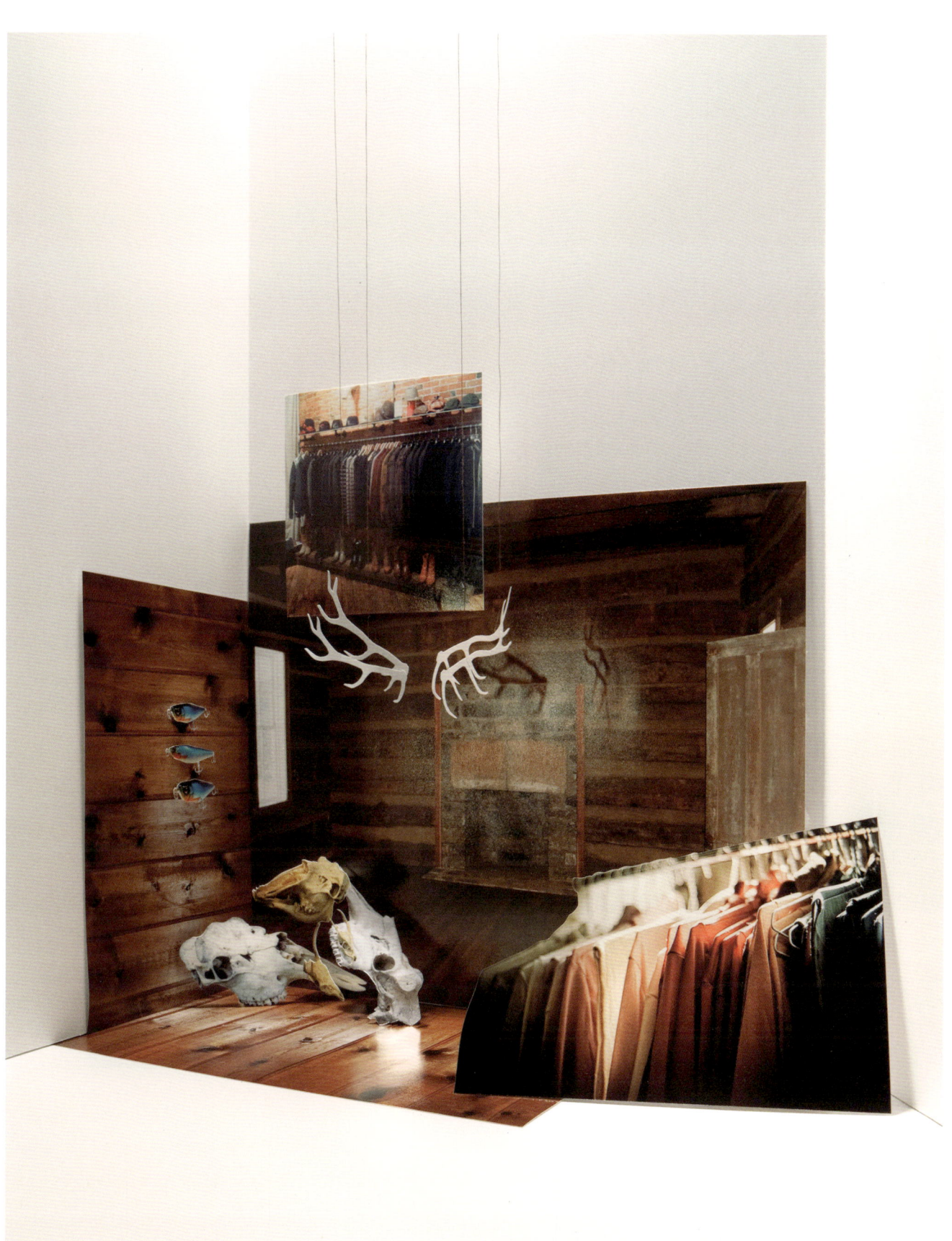

Bennett and I were in a familiar place that had been transformed into something unfamiliar, for a party. It felt like a lucid dream.

With a shrug, he asked, *Have I mentioned that I might love you?*

Fuck no, you didn't mention that.

That summer, I drove eight hours in an unreliable car to see him. We met outside the LL Bean in Freeport so that he could buy fly-fishing lures. I stopped short when I saw two moose skulls in a display case, facing each other. The plaque explained that the skulls had been discovered just like that—two bulls had starved to death after getting their antlers tangled.

When I looked up, I realized that I was alone. Bennett, who'd forgotten to mention that he loved me, had also forgotten that he was with me.

At least I won't starve to death, I thought, and bought a cup of coffee.

I might love you.

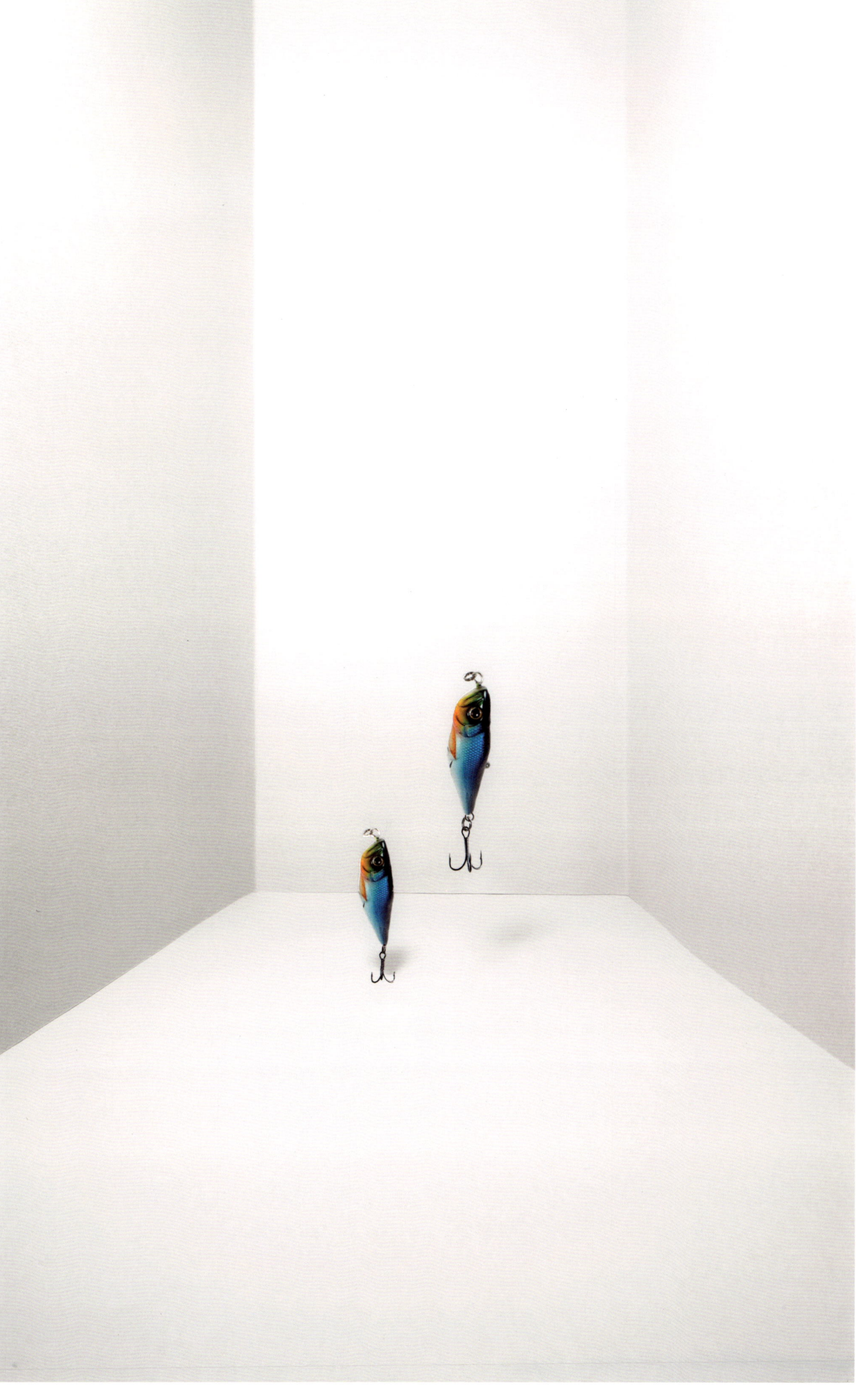

~~Daniel~~
~~Mason~~
~~Hudson~~
~~Spencer~~
~~Conor~~
~~Henry~~
~~Brandon~~
~~Pascal~~
~~Ray~~
~~Jimmy~~
~~Patrick~~
~~Kyle~~
~~Lee~~
~~Naomi~~
~~Kyle, again~~
~~Sam~~
~~Jack~~
~~Tony~~
~~Greg~~
~~Benneth~~

Charlie

I was in an open relationship and Charlie seemed like he wouldn't mind. We left a bar together and walked through a park to get to my house. I snuck him upstairs, not wanting my roommates to question how it was I could be sleeping with someone else. I loved my boyfriend, but we were living in different states at the time. We were doing whatever we could to keep ourselves afloat. My phone rang while I was having sex with Charlie and I tried not to think of my boyfriend on the other end. I didn't want to picture him imagining me with other guys, the way I imagined him with other women every time he didn't answer his phone.

I woke up in the morning with a sense of accomplishment—realizing that I was capable of this arrangement. I had enjoyed my night and knew that I didn't love my boyfriend any less because of it. I wondered how long Charlie and I could go on without upsetting any emotional balances.

Charlie called me later that week, telling me that he'd just been informed by a former fling that he should get tested. He suggested that I do the same. I did, immediately. In the clinic waiting room, I leafed through magazines and tried to shake the thought that I was being punished.

I told Charlie when I found out I was clean. He sounded relieved, but also annoyed. I couldn't believe it when he stopped talking to me at parties.

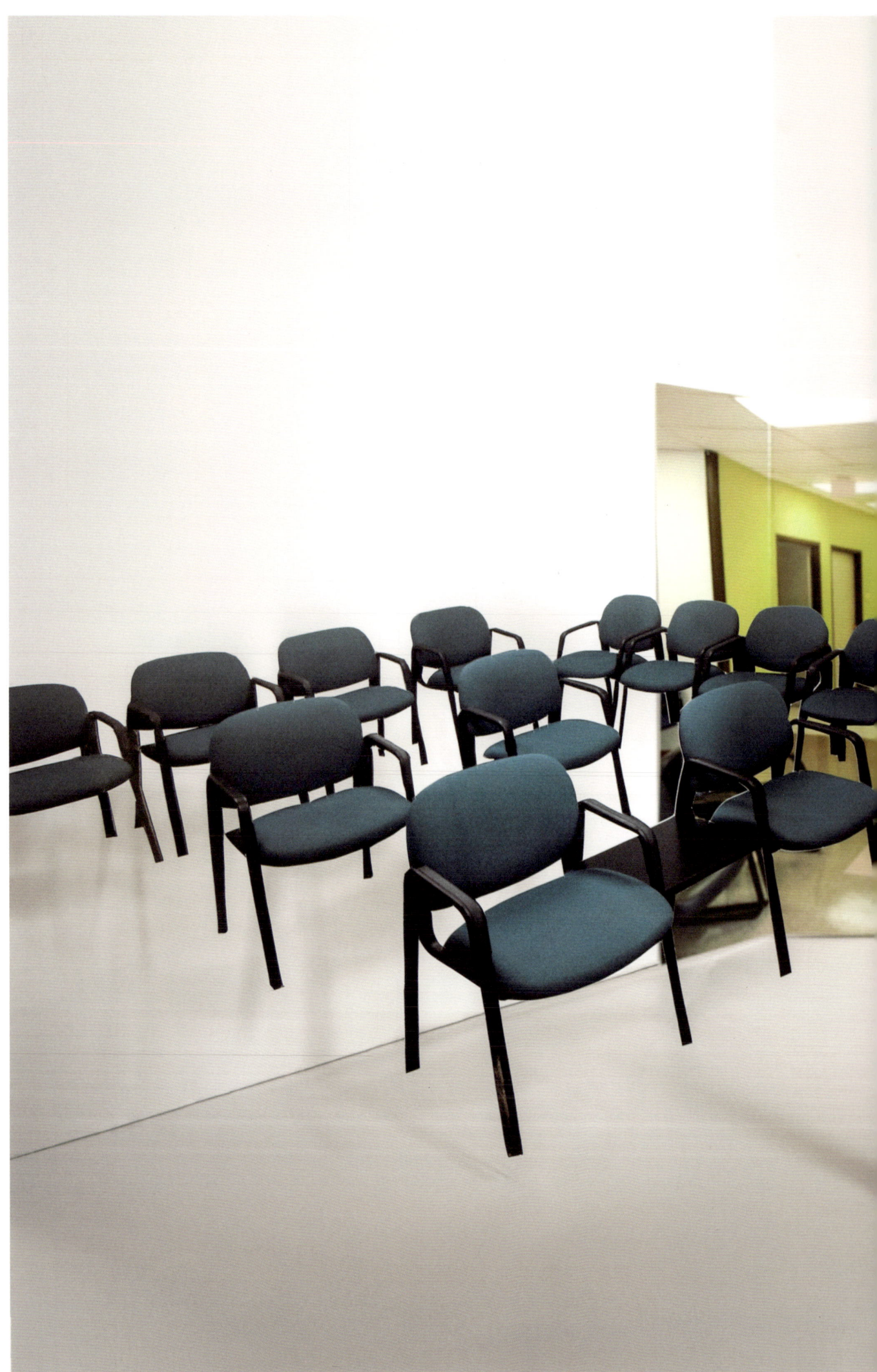

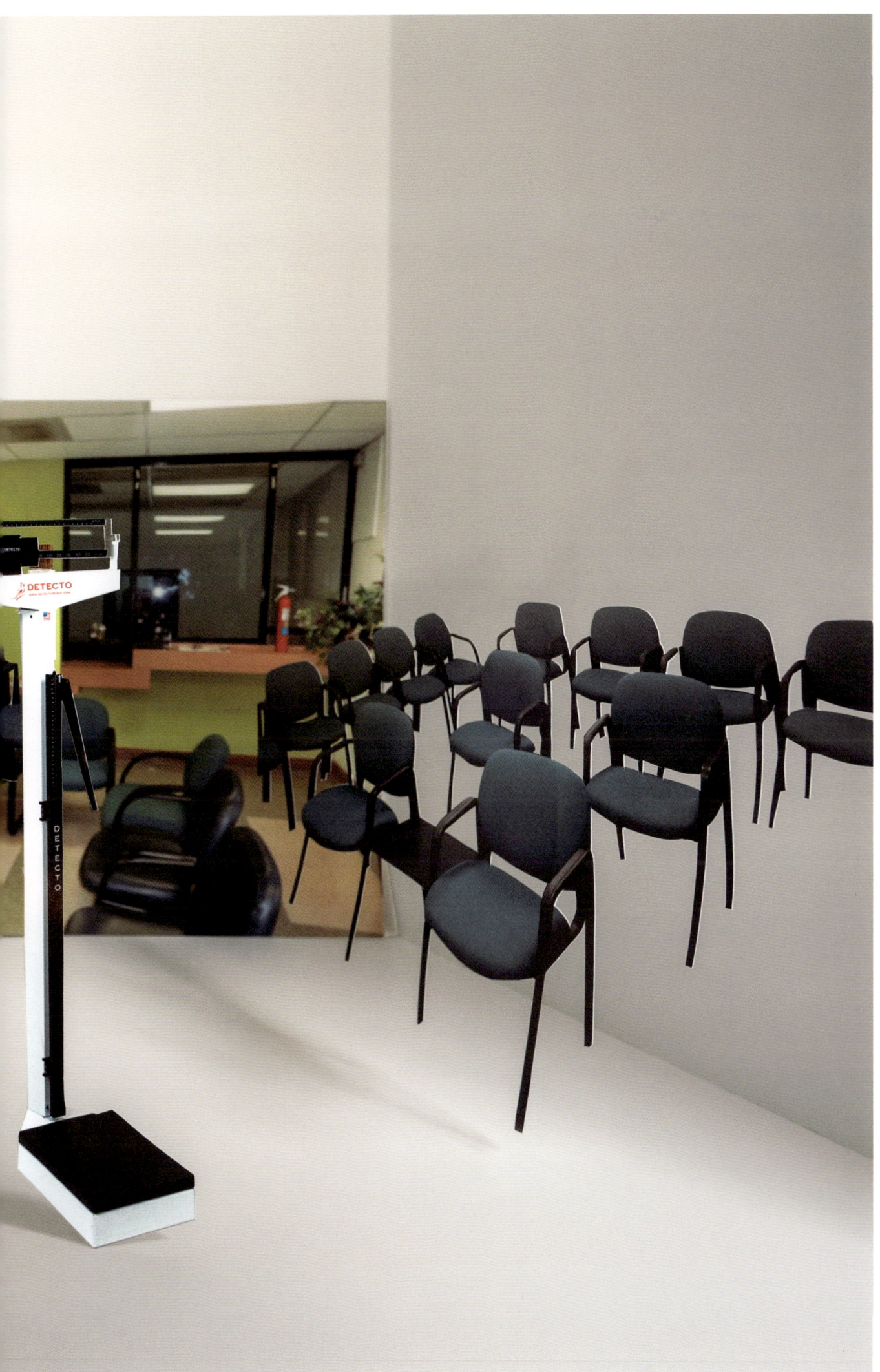

~~Daniel~~
~~Mason~~
~~Hudson~~
~~Spencer~~
~~Conor~~
Henry
~~Brandon~~
~~Pascal~~
~~Ray~~
~~Jimmy~~
Patrick
~~Kyle~~
~~Lee~~
~~Naomi~~
~~Kyle, again~~
~~Sam~~
~~Jack~~
~~Tony~~
~~Greg~~
~~Benneth~~
~~Charlie~~

Milo

I saw Milo around town for months before we ever spoke. All I knew was that he rode a motorcycle and went to the same bar I did. We made eyes at each other sometimes but, until the day he sat down next to me, I had felt like something between us was unbridgeable. I had imagined us speaking dozens of times. I had played out entire relationships in my head. In the fantasies, I was bold and willing.

The first time I heard him speak, his voice surprised me—quieter and more certain than I'd ever thought. He asked me if I'd ever been on a motorcycle. I shook my head no. He told me to go for a ride with him. *You'll like it,* he said. It was as though he were reading the script that I'd written for us in my mind. He hit every line, just right, but when my turn came I stammered and missed my mark. My voice was so meek when I turned him down that I barely recognized it.

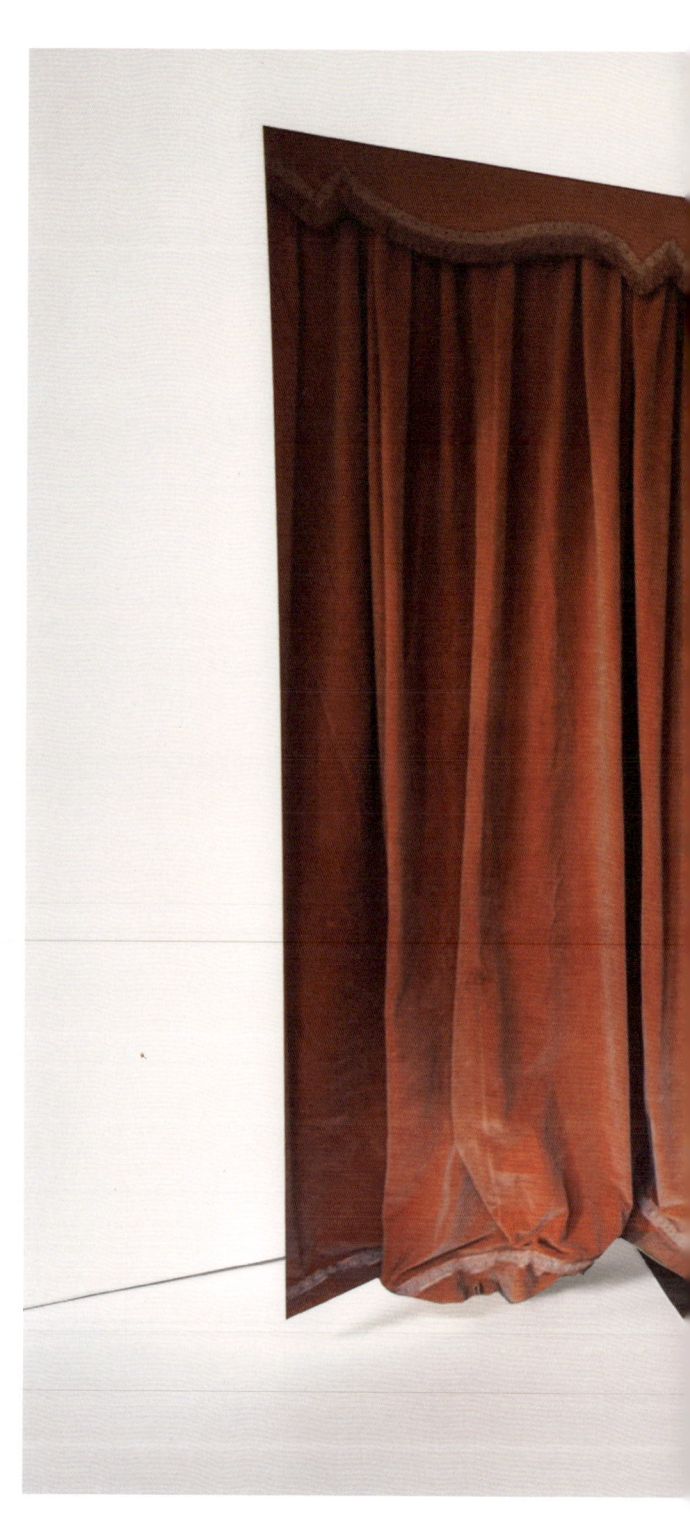

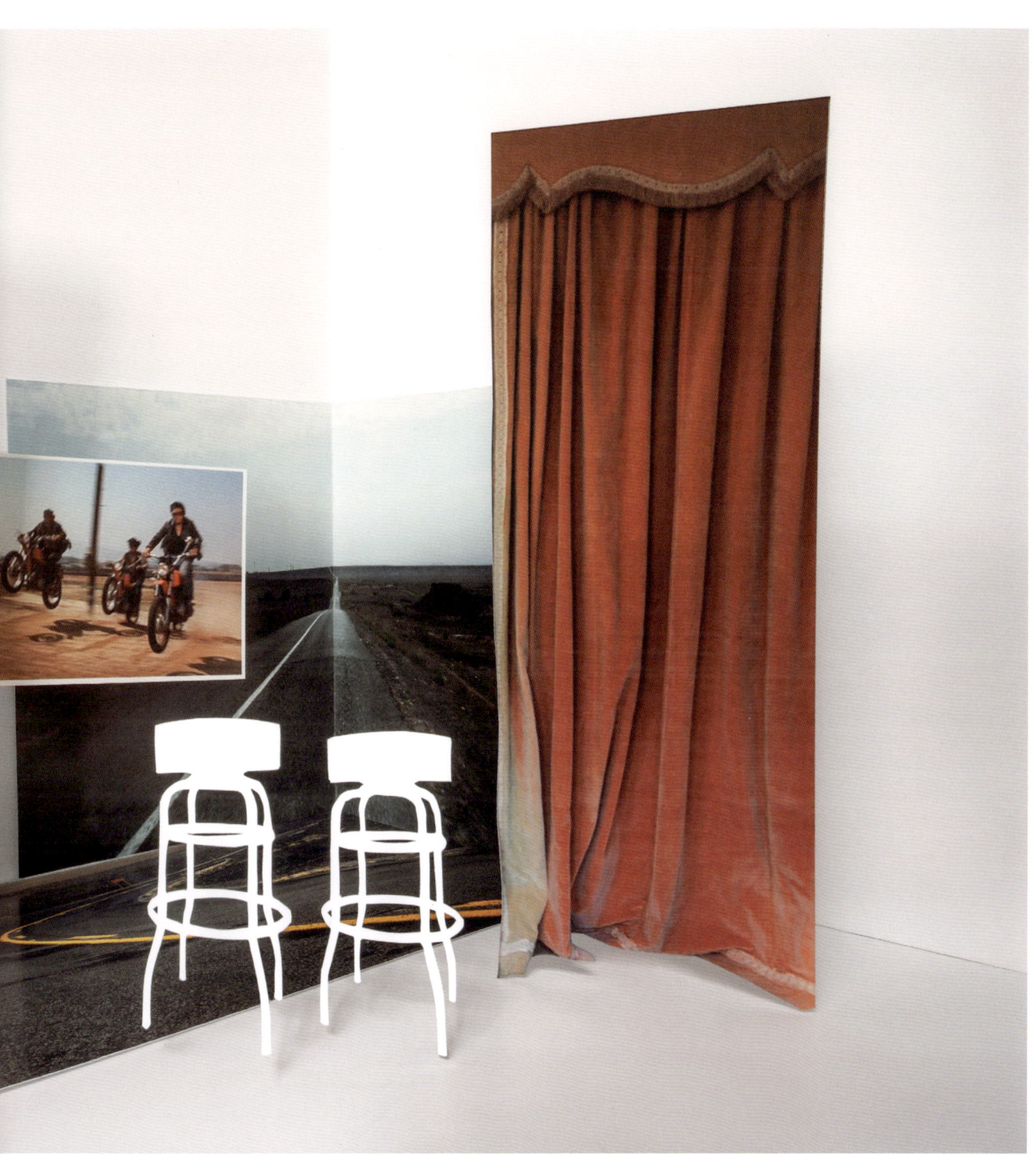

~~Daniel~~
~~Mason~~
~~Hudson~~
~~Spencer~~
~~Conor~~
~~Henry~~
~~Brandon~~
~~Pascal~~
~~Ray~~
~~Jimmy~~
~~Patrick~~
~~Kyle~~
~~Lee~~
~~Naomi~~
~~Kyle, again~~
~~Sam~~
~~Jack~~
~~Tony~~
~~Greg~~
~~Bennett~~
~~Charlie~~
~~Milo~~

Durant

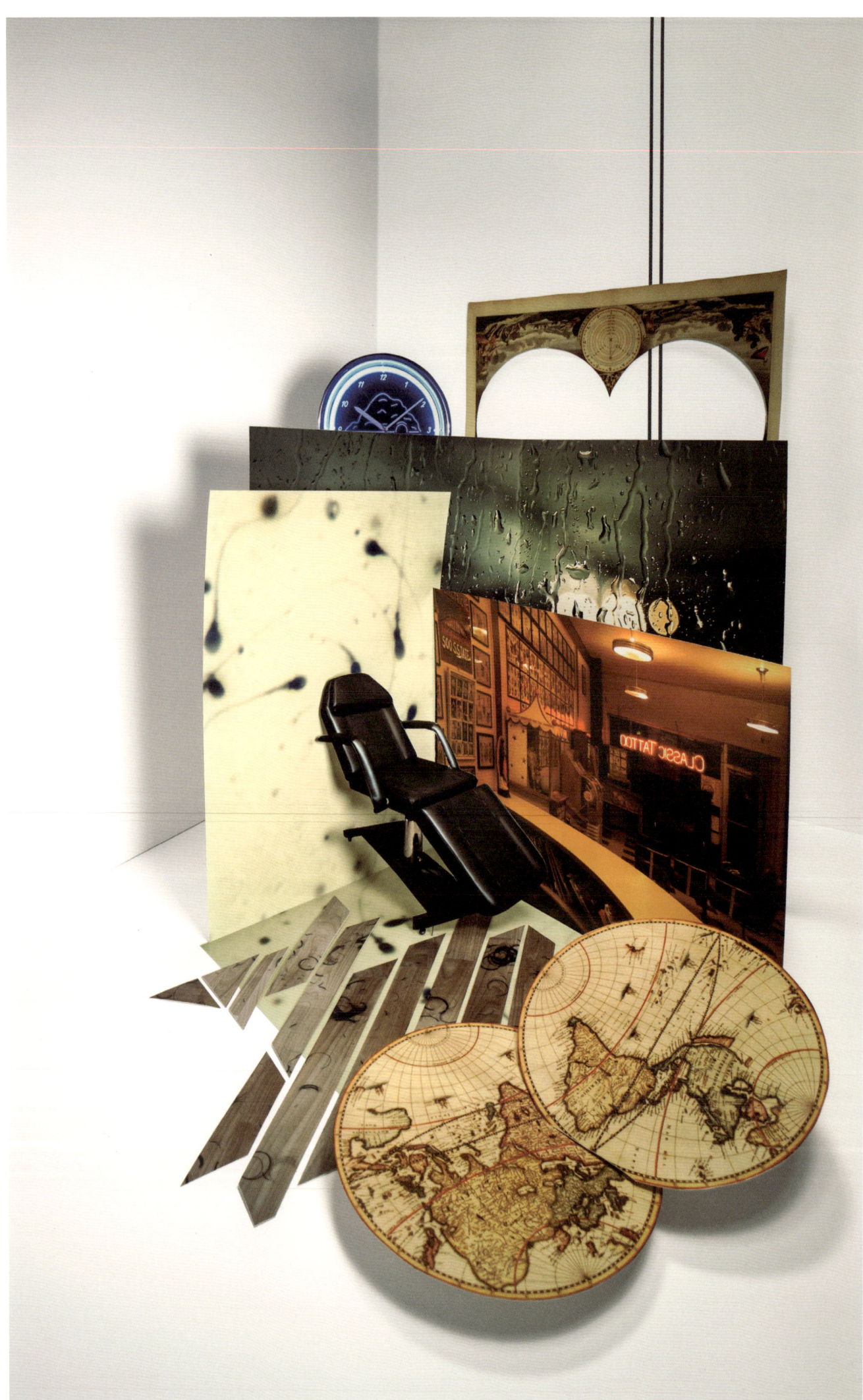

Durant was older and had wanted to get me pregnant the first time that we slept together. He said that I'd be a great mother. He wanted to be a young, cool dad. I wanted to travel. I had plans. I asked him to wait. *Wait for me, please,* I would say, and he did, for years.

He turned thirty and it tore him apart. I wasn't enough to make him feel young anymore. He wanted a baby. A wife. He wanted it to be me, but another woman would do. I needed to move again and he wouldn't come with me. *Please, just wait for me. A few more years. You have time.* He said that he was done waiting. He begged me to stay, to settle down. I couldn't, so I left.

We reacted to the breakup like teenagers. I cut my hair and he shaved his head. We both got tattoos. He got his nose pierced. Despite everything, I didn't think it was possible for us to move on. I never thought that it would stick. Even as we both began seeing other people, I still believed, deeply, that we would find our way back to each other.

~~Daniel~~
~~Mason~~
~~Hudson~~
~~Spencer~~
~~Conor~~
~~Henry~~
~~Brandon~~
~~Pascal~~
~~Ray~~
~~Jimmy~~
~~Patrick~~
~~Kyle~~
~~Lee~~
~~Naomi~~
~~Kyle, again~~
~~Sam~~
~~Jack~~
~~Tony~~
~~Greg~~
~~Bennett~~
~~Charlie~~
~~Milo~~
~~Durant~~

Scott

Scott was younger than me and eager to please. I'd picked him up at a bar. He was a trombone player built like an athlete. We never ate dinner together. We never met each other's friends. He came over one night and the buzzer to my apartment was broken. I had to walk down five flights to let him in. It felt like such a bother.

The next morning, standing in my hallway, I kissed Scott more sweetly than I ever had. He had nice eyes that I'd never noticed. *I'm going to miss you,* I told him.

Why?

Because I'm never going to see you again.

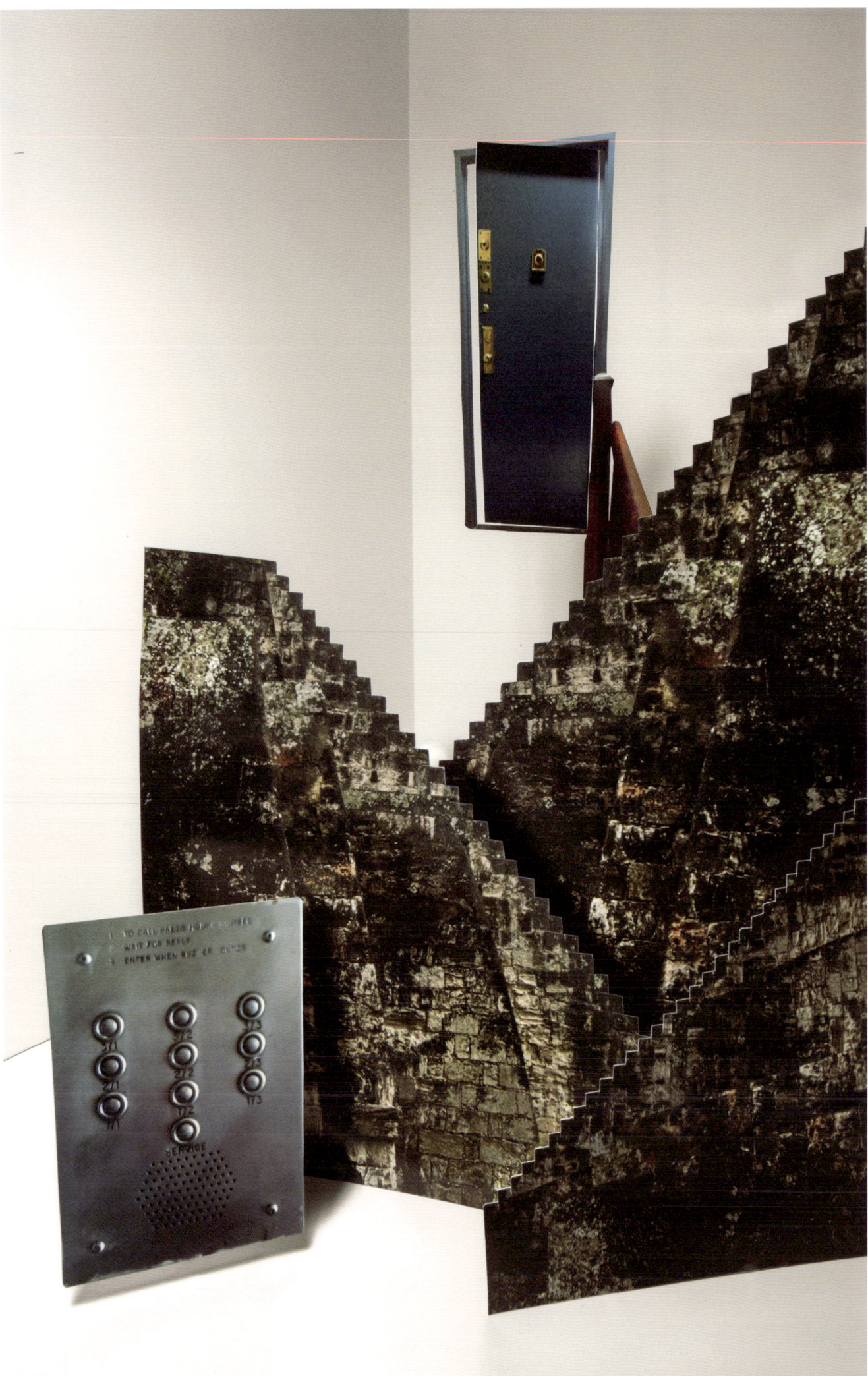

~~Daniel~~
~~Mason~~
~~Hudson~~
~~Spencer~~
~~Conor~~
~~Henry~~
~~Brandon~~
~~Pascal~~
~~Ray~~
~~Jimmy~~
~~Patrick~~
~~Kyle~~
~~Lee~~
~~Naomi~~
~~Kyle, again~~
~~Sam~~
~~Jack~~
~~Tony~~
~~Greg~~
~~Bennett~~
~~Charlie~~
~~Milo~~
~~Durant~~
~~Scott~~

Will

Will drove his car everywhere. The only time that I ever saw him ride the subway, he refused to sit down on the orange plastic seats. I didn't understand how you could make it through New York City being a germaphobe, but he managed somehow. He told me that I'd be lucky to meet another guy in New York with a car. We were down by the Gowanus Canal and I didn't feel lucky.

Walking through an industrial complex, Will explained that he'd just gotten out of a messy relationship and wanted to take things slowly. I told him that I was in the same place, even though mine had ended months ago. We both seemed to be saying that we would try, but not cling.

When Will got drunk, which was often, he could get it up but never come. We developed a routine—sex at night for me, and then again in the morning, for him. One day, he woke up early and left before getting his. He told me that he had *things to do*, but we both knew what he meant.

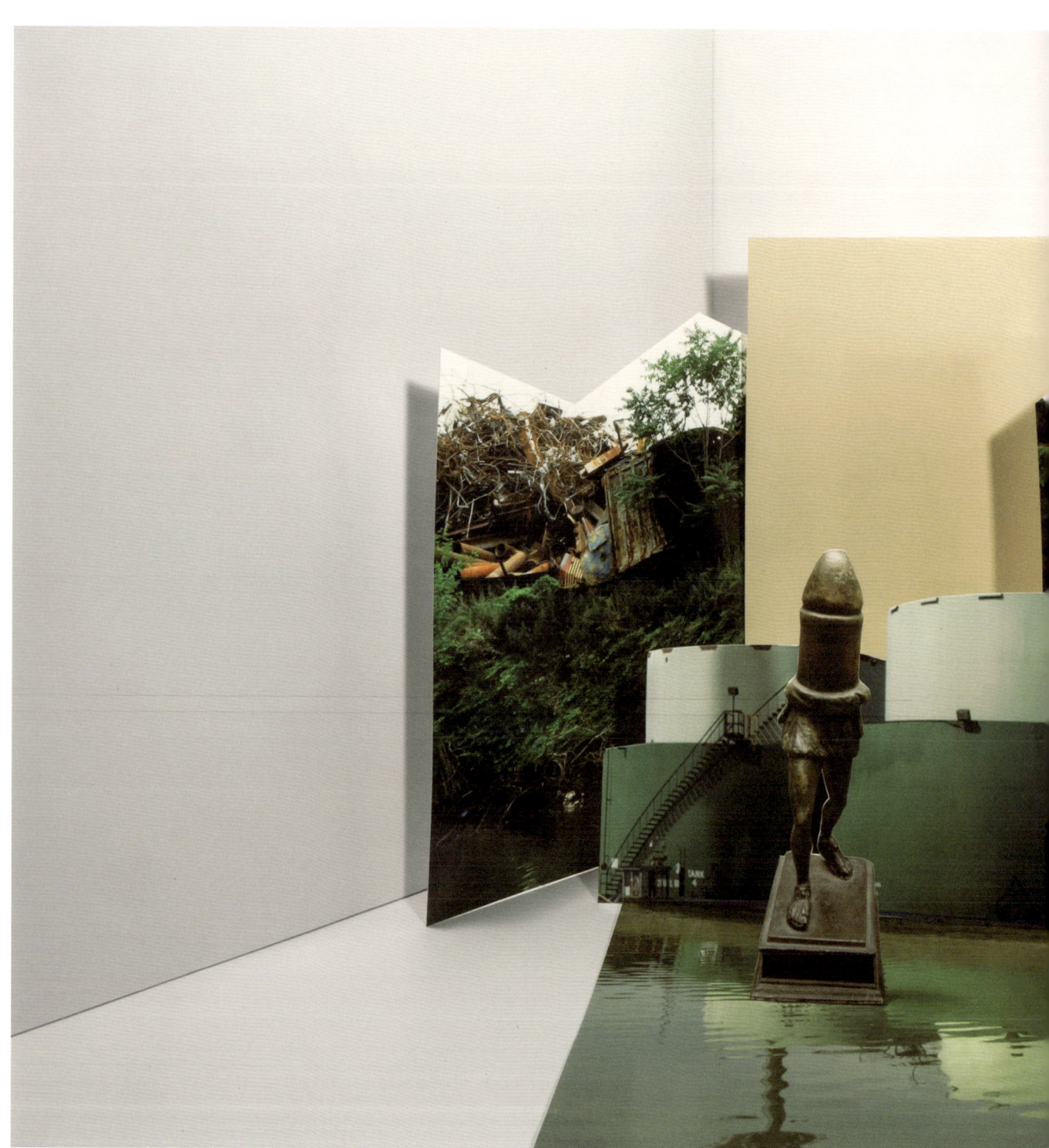

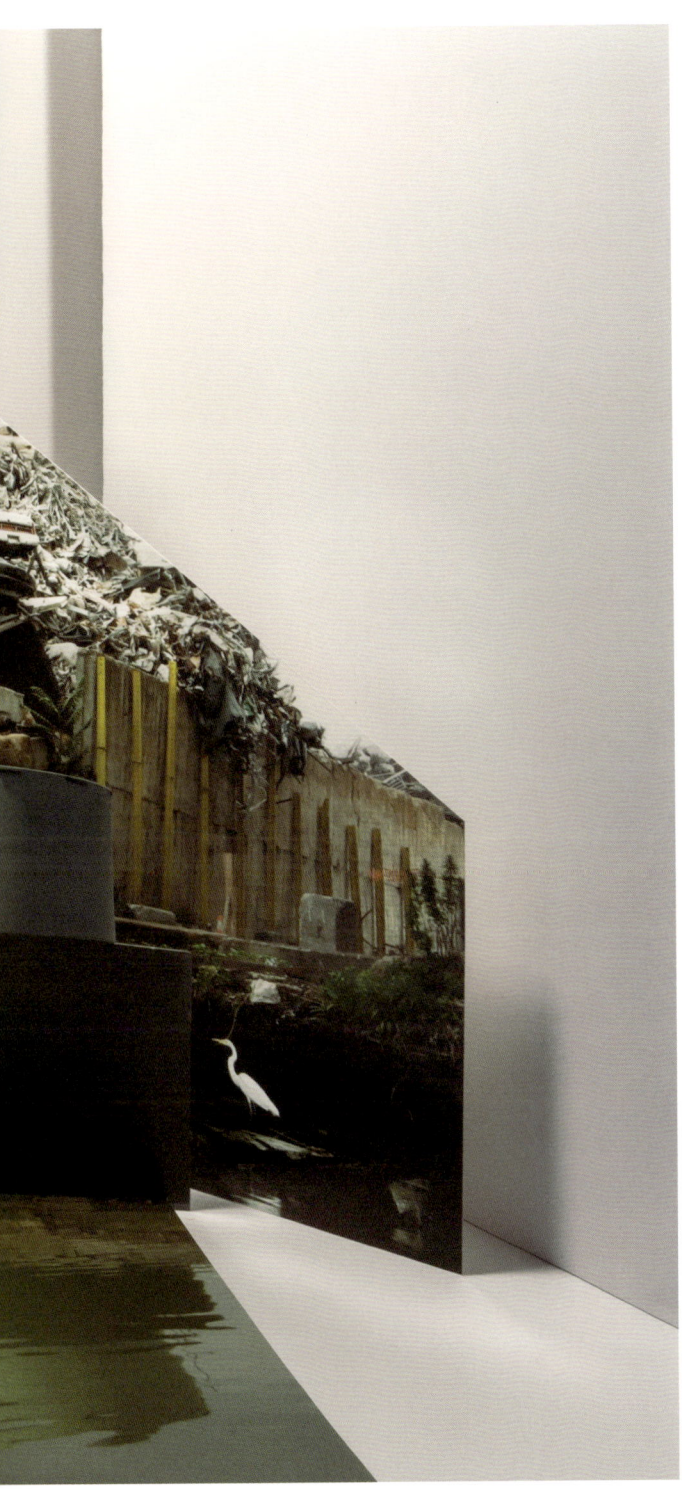

~~Daniel~~
~~Mason~~
~~Hudson~~
~~Spencer~~
~~Conor~~
~~Henry~~
~~Brandon~~
~~Pascal~~
~~Ray~~
~~Jimmy~~
~~Patrick~~
~~Kyle~~
~~Lee~~
~~Naomi~~
~~Kyle, again~~
~~Sam~~
~~Jack~~
~~Tony~~
~~Greg~~
~~Bennett~~
~~Charlie~~
~~Milo~~
~~Durant~~
~~Scott~~
~~Will~~

Durant, again

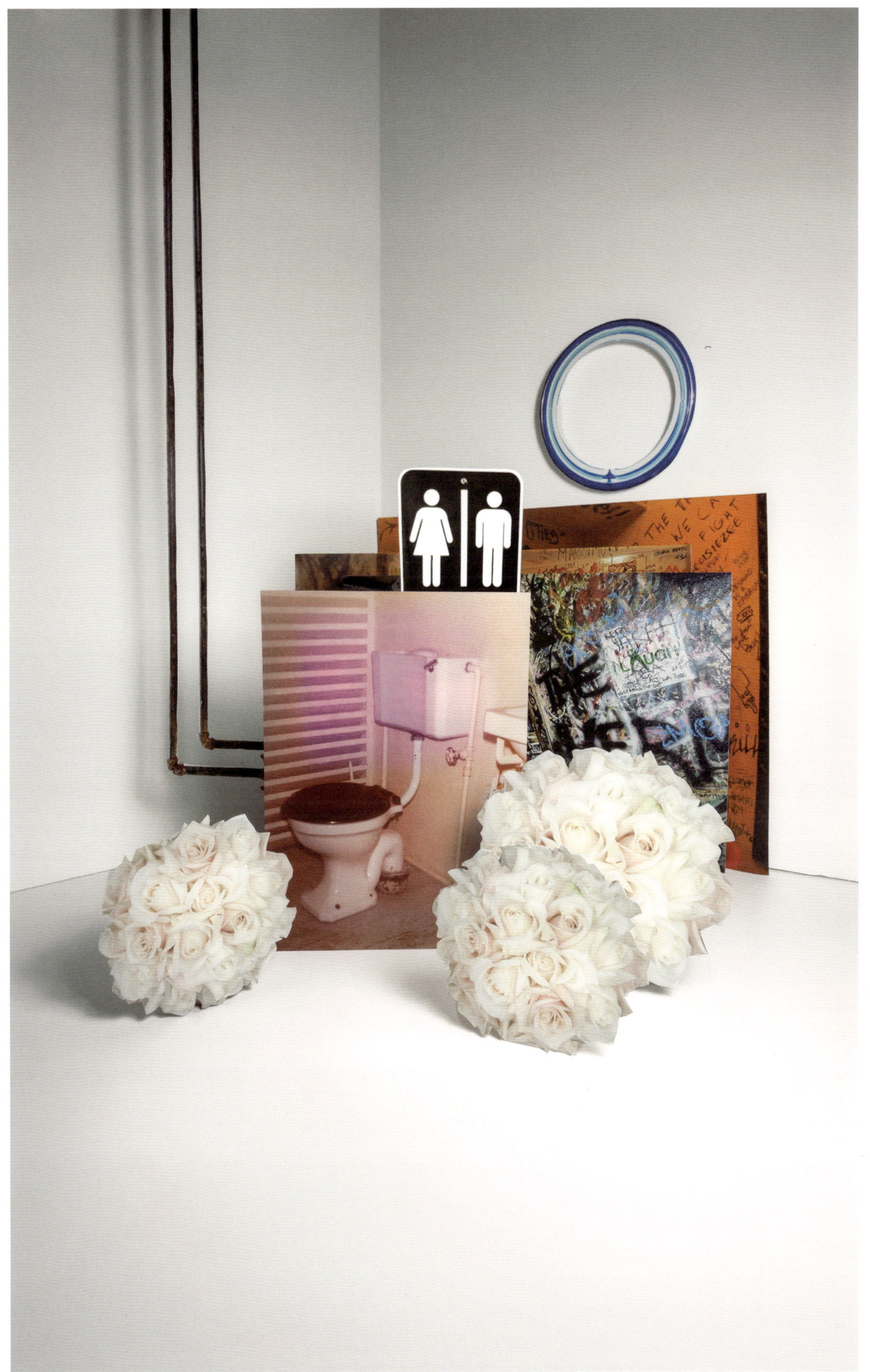

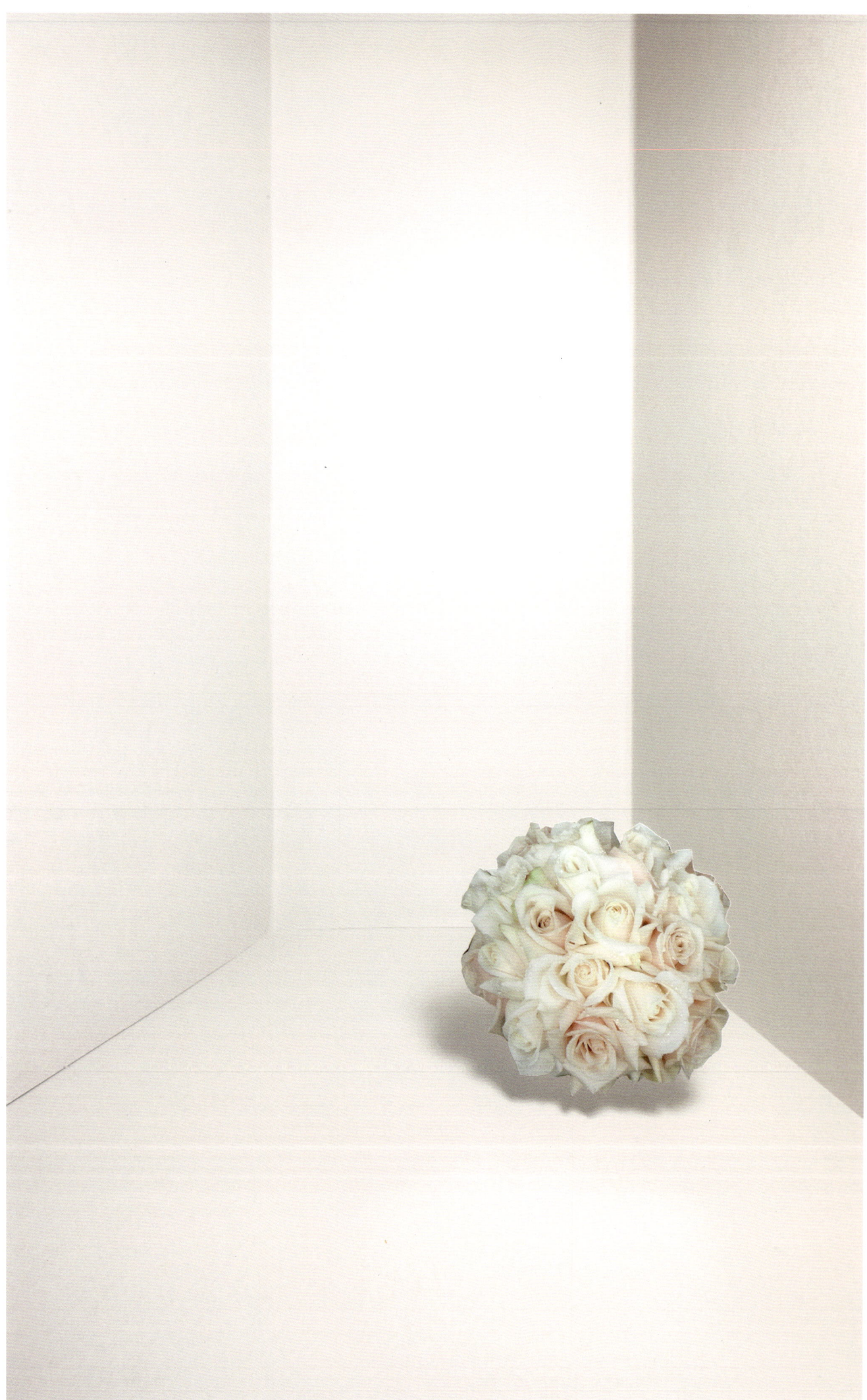

Durant got engaged six months after I moved away. The night I found out, I called up my Russian friend, who I knew wouldn't ask questions, and told him that I needed to drink. We met at a dive bar that played only punk. I drank straight whiskey until I threw up in the dirty bathroom. My friend had to walk me home and put me to bed. I took my shirt off and showed him my tattoo, wanting to think it was worth something.

For a while, I expected Durant to call and tell me that it was a joke—a desperate ploy to have me come back to him. He went through with it, though. I heard that part of his wedding vows described love as not being a feeling, but *a decision you make.*

~~Daniel~~
~~Mason~~
~~Hudson~~
~~Spencer~~
~~Conor~~
Henry
~~Brandon~~
~~Pascal~~
~~Ray~~
~~Jimmy~~
Patrick
~~Kyle~~
~~Lee~~
~~Naomi~~
Kyle, again
~~Sam~~
~~Jack~~
~~Tony~~
~~Greg~~
~~Bennett~~
~~Charlie~~
~~Milo~~
~~Durant~~
Scott
~~Will~~
~~Durant, again~~

Nikolai

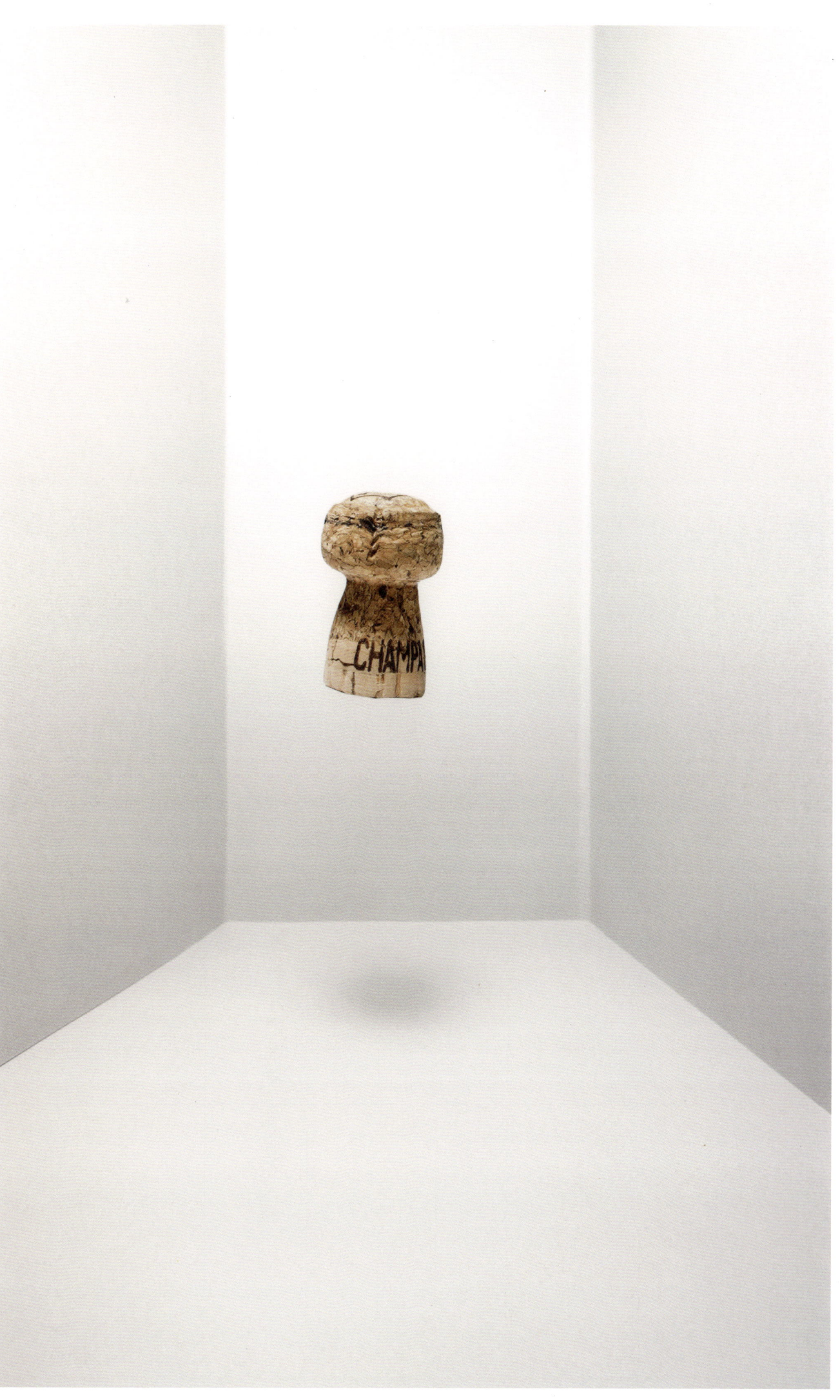

Nikolai lived in my neighborhood. We were drinking buddies. He had a girlfriend in China. There seemed to be a countdown to when she would finally arrive, but it was delayed, month by month. She didn't come, and we got closer, stayed out longer, drank more. Some nights we were just friends. Other nights we kissed. Each time, it surprised me. When I let him, he would fall asleep on my bed, fully clothed. I think he would have spent every night with me, like that, but I usually kicked him out, clinging to some slippery boundary.

His girlfriend finally booked a flight. I wasn't sure whether it was guilt or the thought of losing what I had with Nikolai, but I dreaded meeting her. The week of her flight, she was hit in the eye by a champagne cork. She canceled her trip, delaying another month. Nikolai invited me to a party that night and neither of us said much, but it felt like celebrating.

We drank more than we ever had. He kissed me in a bar, surrounded by friends who knew about his girlfriend. I was the one who suggested we leave, trying to protect his relationship. Outside, we hooked up on the street. It was different. He shoved his arm down my jeans and he didn't feel like a friend anymore. When we stumbled to the front of his apartment, he stopped short, as if realizing what we were about to do. He frowned at me and looked at his feet. *Now it's awkward,* was all he could say.

Now? I said. *Now it's awkward?* I stormed off, hating both of us and his girlfriend. When she finally did arrive, Nikolai and I stopped drinking together.

I still run into them sometimes and she won't look me in the eye.

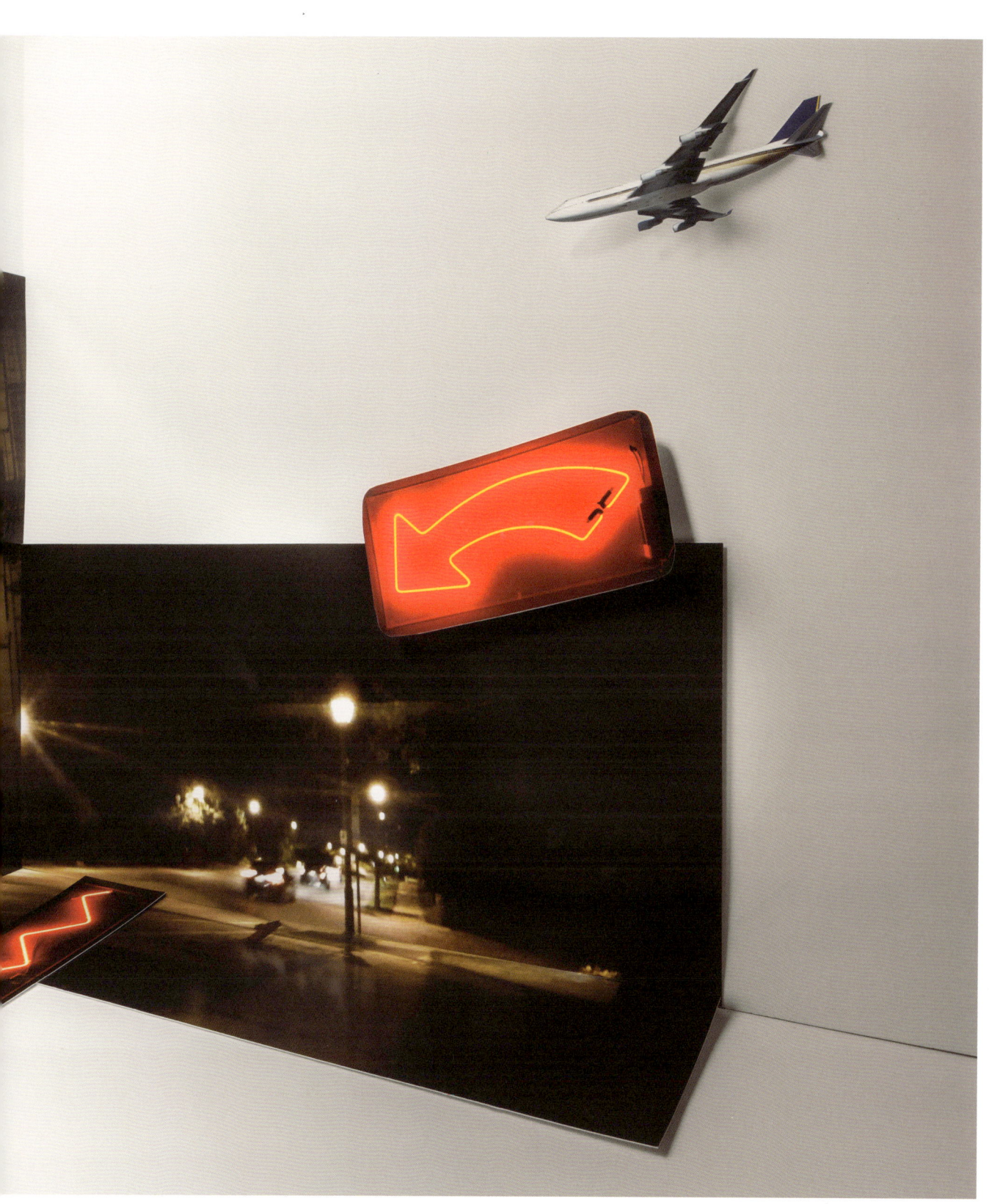

~~Daniel~~
~~Mason~~
~~Hudson~~
~~Spencer~~
~~Conor~~
~~Henry~~
~~Brandon~~
~~Pascal~~
~~Ray~~
~~Jimmy~~
~~Patrick~~
~~Kyle~~
~~Lee~~
~~Naomi~~
~~Kyle, again~~
~~Sam~~
~~Jack~~
~~Tony~~
~~Greg~~
~~Bennett~~
~~Charlie~~
~~Milo~~
~~Durant~~
~~Scott~~
~~Will~~
~~Durant, again~~
~~Nikolai~~

John

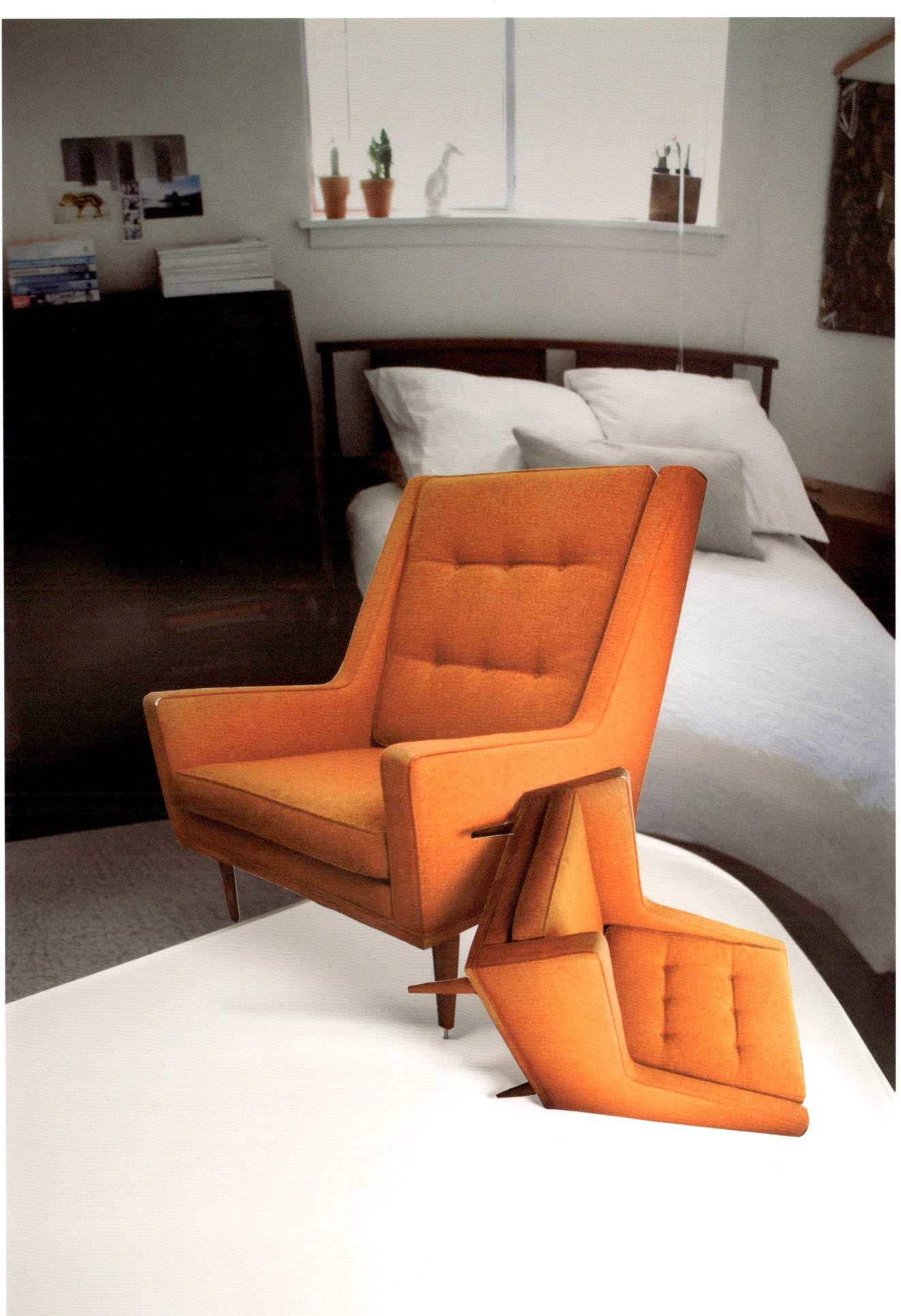

Sometimes John felt so blank that I suspected a terrible thing had happened to him as a child—something that he'd blocked completely. I found myself suspicious of anyone that he'd admired as a boy—family members, coaches, teachers. It's likely, though, that I was making something out of nothing.

You never write about me, he complained.

Maybe you're not very interesting, I posited.

Oh really? he asked, sweeping a pile of books off my nightstand and then another, off my dresser. When he was done, he sat on the ugly, orange armchair—heaving and triumphant.

I stood up. *I'm going to take a shower.* When I got back to the room, John had returned everything exactly where it had been.

Maybe you're not very interesting.

~~Daniel~~
~~Mason~~
~~Hudson~~
~~Spencer~~
~~Conor~~
~~Henry~~
~~Brandon~~
~~Pascal~~
~~Ray~~
~~Jimmy~~
~~Patrick~~
~~Kyle~~
~~Lee~~
~~Naomi~~
~~Kyle, again~~
~~Sam~~
~~Jack~~
~~Tony~~
~~Greg~~
~~Bennett~~
~~Charlie~~
~~Milo~~
~~Durant~~
~~Scott~~
~~Will~~
~~Durant, again~~
~~Nikolai~~
~~John~~

Carlos

Carlos was religious the way that I was a Knicks fan—it was something he'd been born into but knew nothing about. At night, he got so drunk that he whispered to me in Spanish, forgetting that I couldn't understand. We miscommunicated about everything, but I knew he loved me because I could feel it. When I got the flu, I stayed at his apartment for five days. He had all my shifts covered and brought me soup every night. He told me that his mother had prayed for me. It was the only time that hasn't made me uncomfortable.

Carlos was stabbed in the knees when he was eleven, waiting for a bus. His cousin had been shot. His father was missing. I shouldn't have been surprised when Carlos was arrested, but I was. The cops tried to get me to say that my car had been stolen. They could have impounded it, but instead brought me back the keys, having assumed that Carlos had been lying when he said the white girl on the registration was his girlfriend. The moment I saw the cops, I could feel that we were over, but I couldn't leave yet. I visited him in jail, using a corded phone to talk to him through Plexiglas. I felt like I had fallen asleep during a movie—completely unsure of how I'd gotten where I was.

I stayed with him long enough to bail him out, get him back home, help him find another job. I played the part as best I could, but Carlos knew the whole time that I was leaving him.

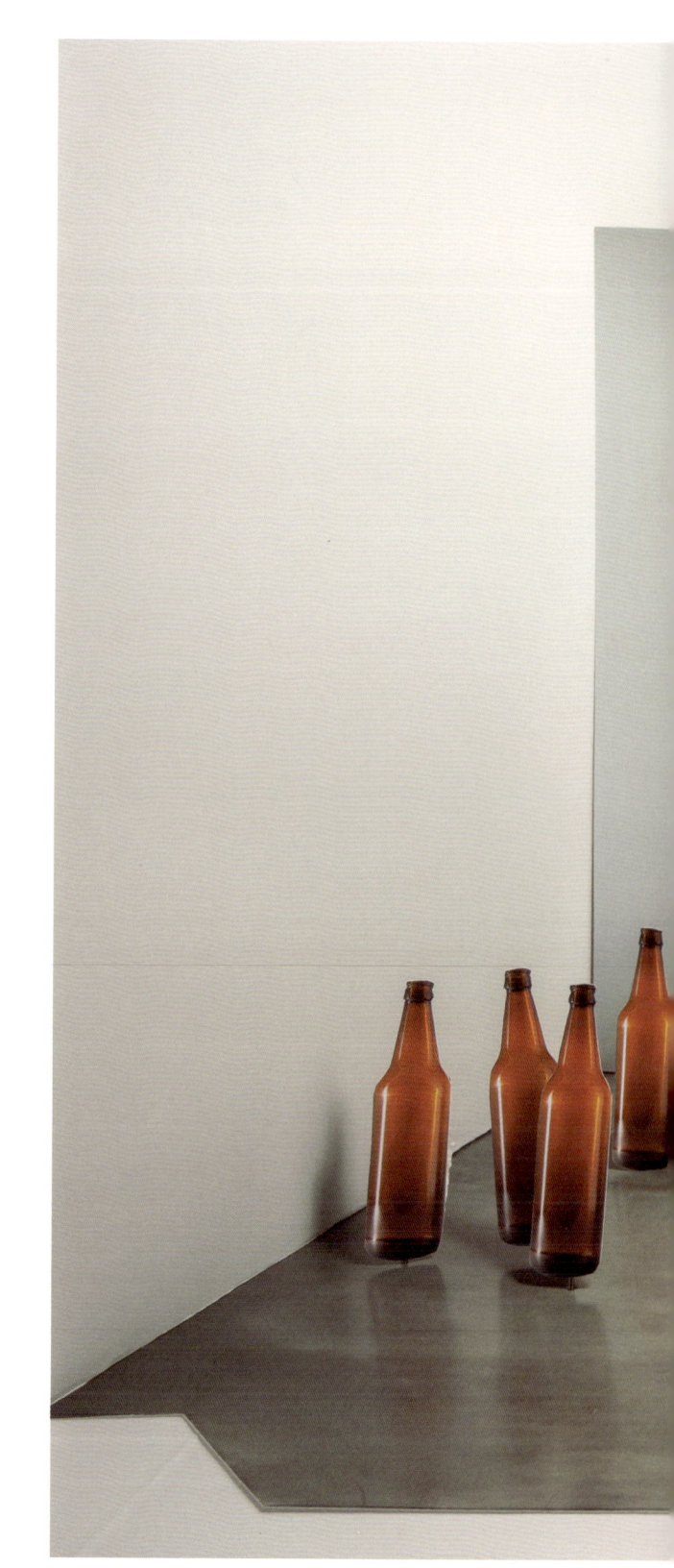

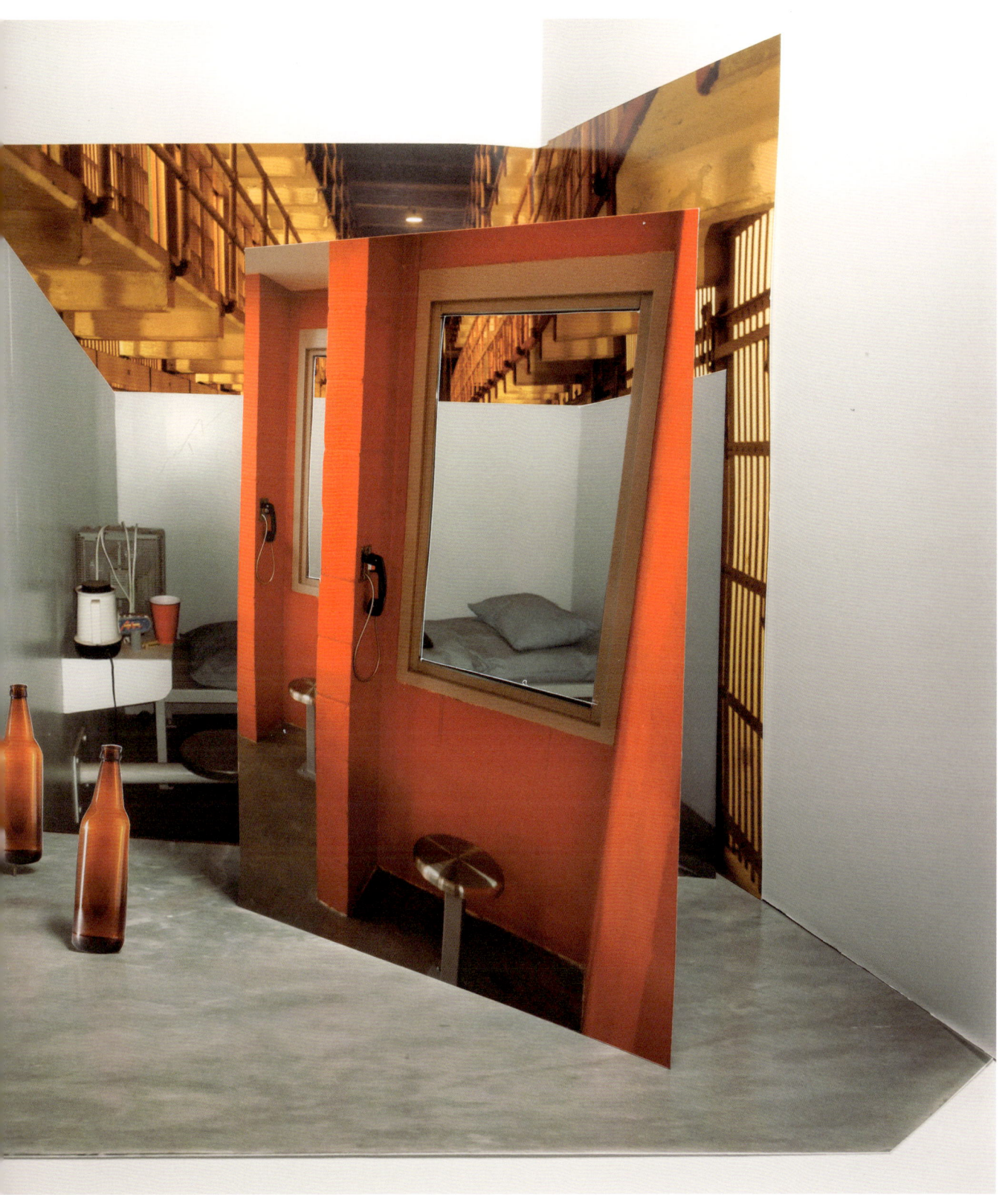

~~Daniel~~
~~Mason~~
~~Hudson~~
~~Spencer~~
~~Conor~~
~~Henry~~
~~Brandon~~
~~Pascal~~
~~Ray~~
~~Jimmy~~
~~Patrick~~
~~Kyle~~
~~Lee~~
~~Naomi~~
~~Kyle, again~~
~~Sam~~
~~Jack~~
~~Tony~~
~~Greg~~
~~Bennett~~
~~Charlie~~
~~Milo~~
~~Durant~~
~~Scott~~
~~Will~~
~~Durant, again~~
~~Nikolai~~
~~John~~
~~Carlos~~

Mike

We had mutual friends but had almost never spoken until Mike came up to me at a bar on St. Patrick's Day. *Do you want to go?* he asked, without any humor. I almost spit. I told him that I was having fun. I kept on dancing. When he came back and asked again, two hours later, I said, *Sure. Let's go.*

Outside, I asked where we were going. *Your place*, he said. I waited for him to laugh, but he didn't. In my bedroom, we were talking about how much we'd both had to drink when Mike started taking off his pants. We hadn't even kissed. I went to get water and when I came back, he was in my bed. We had sex and I thought about how much of my life was powered by momentum.

Mike had to wake up early. I stayed in bed while he got dressed. Once his shoes were on, he smiled. He walked toward the bed with his right arm raised. Reflexively, I high-fived him. All day, I wondered what had just happened.

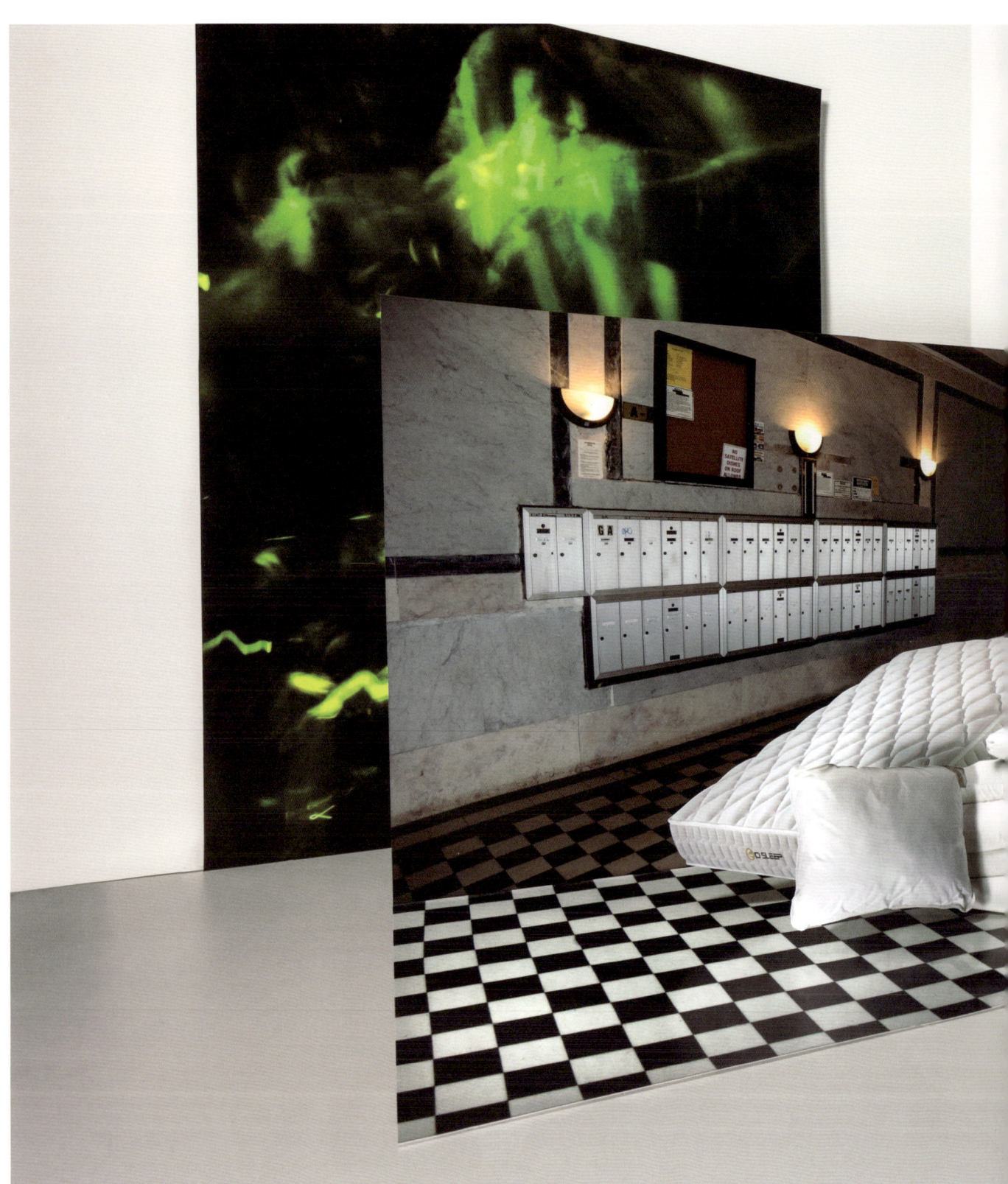

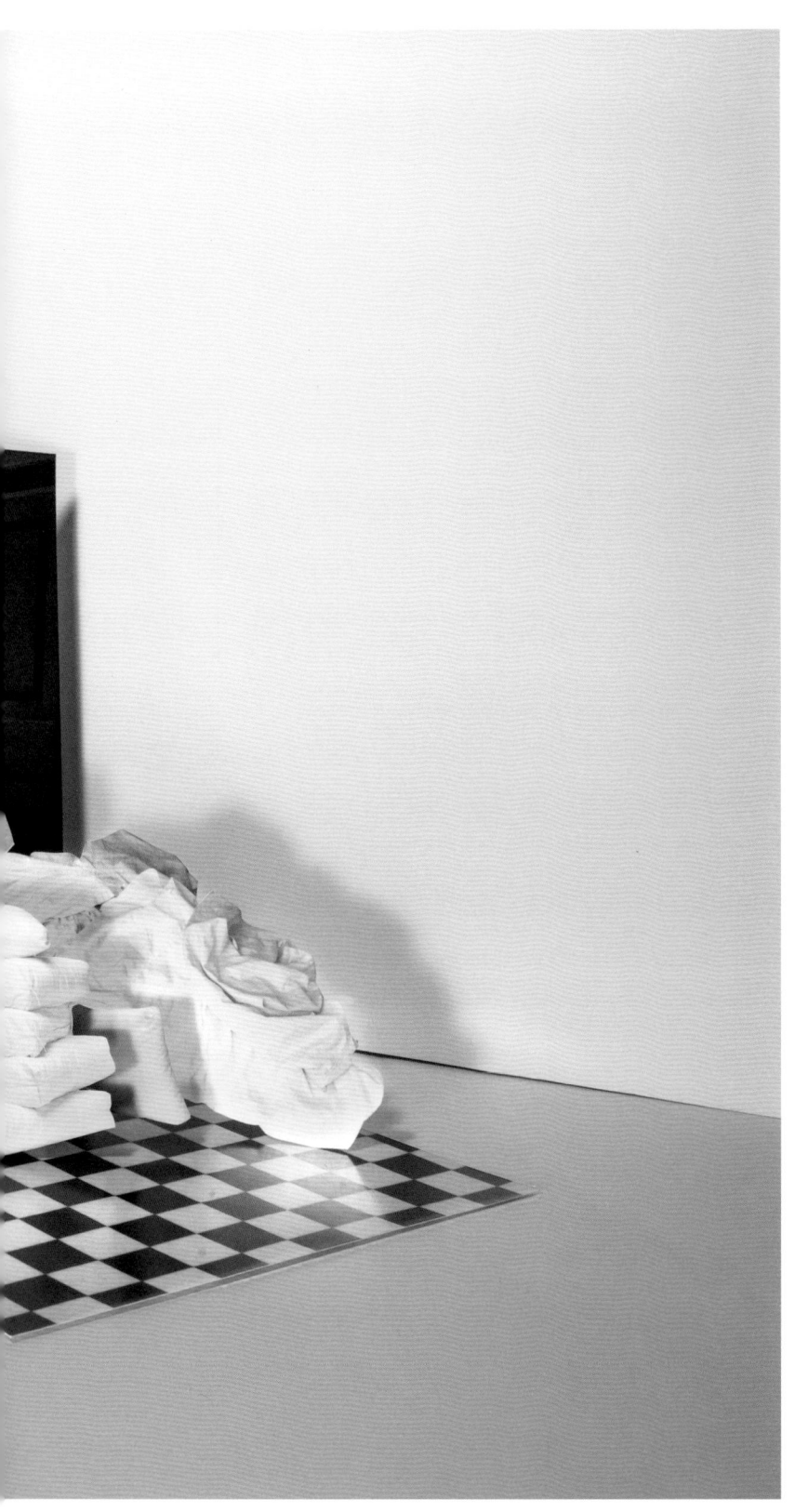

~~Daniel~~
~~Mason~~
~~Hudson~~
~~Spencer~~
~~Conor~~
~~Henry~~
~~Brandon~~
~~Pascal~~
~~Ray~~
~~Jimmy~~
~~Patrick~~
~~Kyle~~
~~Lee~~
~~Naomi~~
~~Kyle, again~~
~~Sam~~
~~Jack~~
~~Tony~~
~~Greg~~
~~Bennett~~
~~Charlie~~
~~Milo~~
~~Durant~~
~~Scott~~
~~Will~~
~~Durant, again~~
~~Nikolai~~
~~John~~
~~Carlos~~
~~Mike~~

Lukas

Lukas and I were in the back of a cab, coming home from a party. He slid his palms toward me, across the leather bench seat, and whispered that he was falling in love with me. We'd only been together for three months and he had been traveling for at least one of them. I still felt as though we barely knew each other.

I was suspicious of his goodness. He hid notes in my bag for me to discover at work. He bought me flowers and made me breakfast. He always walked me home, switching sides along the way to place himself between me and traffic. He folded his underwear and was never late. I wanted to believe that he could fall in love with me so quickly but I didn't. He had to be lying, or at least mistaken. It was winter. My skin was dry and work had given me an ulcer. My hair was growing out at awkward angles. I was distracted. I wasn't my best self.

That night, in his loft bed, Lukas snored and rumbled and spoke. I tried not to listen, but I heard it clear as day when he said again that he loved me. I could have loved him maybe, but it would have taken me years and he never would have had the patience. I wanted to forget the whole thing. I tried to go back to sleep, but couldn't. The sun would be coming up soon. I felt panic spread through my chest. I willed the ladder not to creak as I snuck out of the bed. I grabbed all my stuff, careful not to forget anything.

He called and called, looking for an explanation, but I never had one.

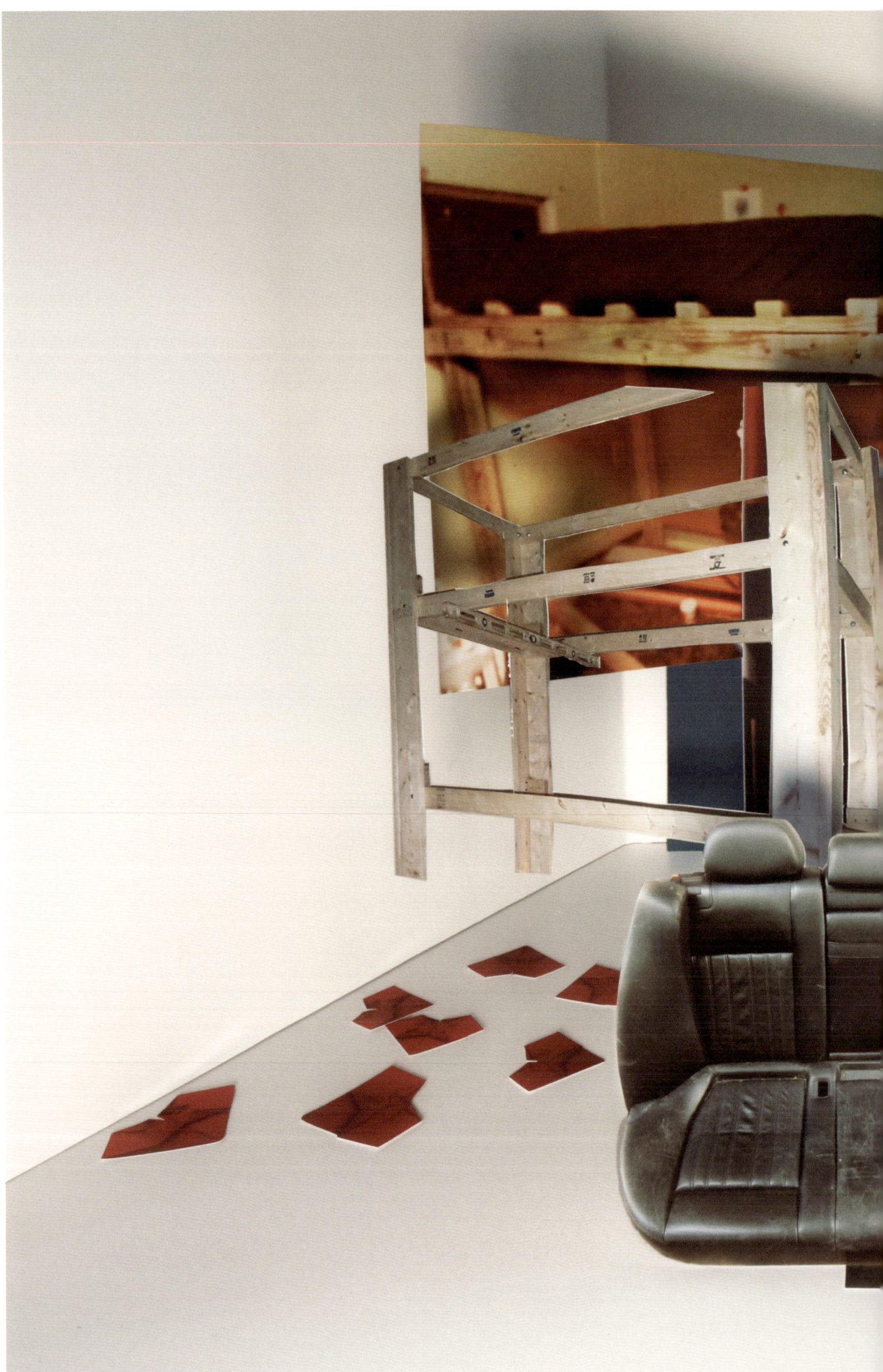

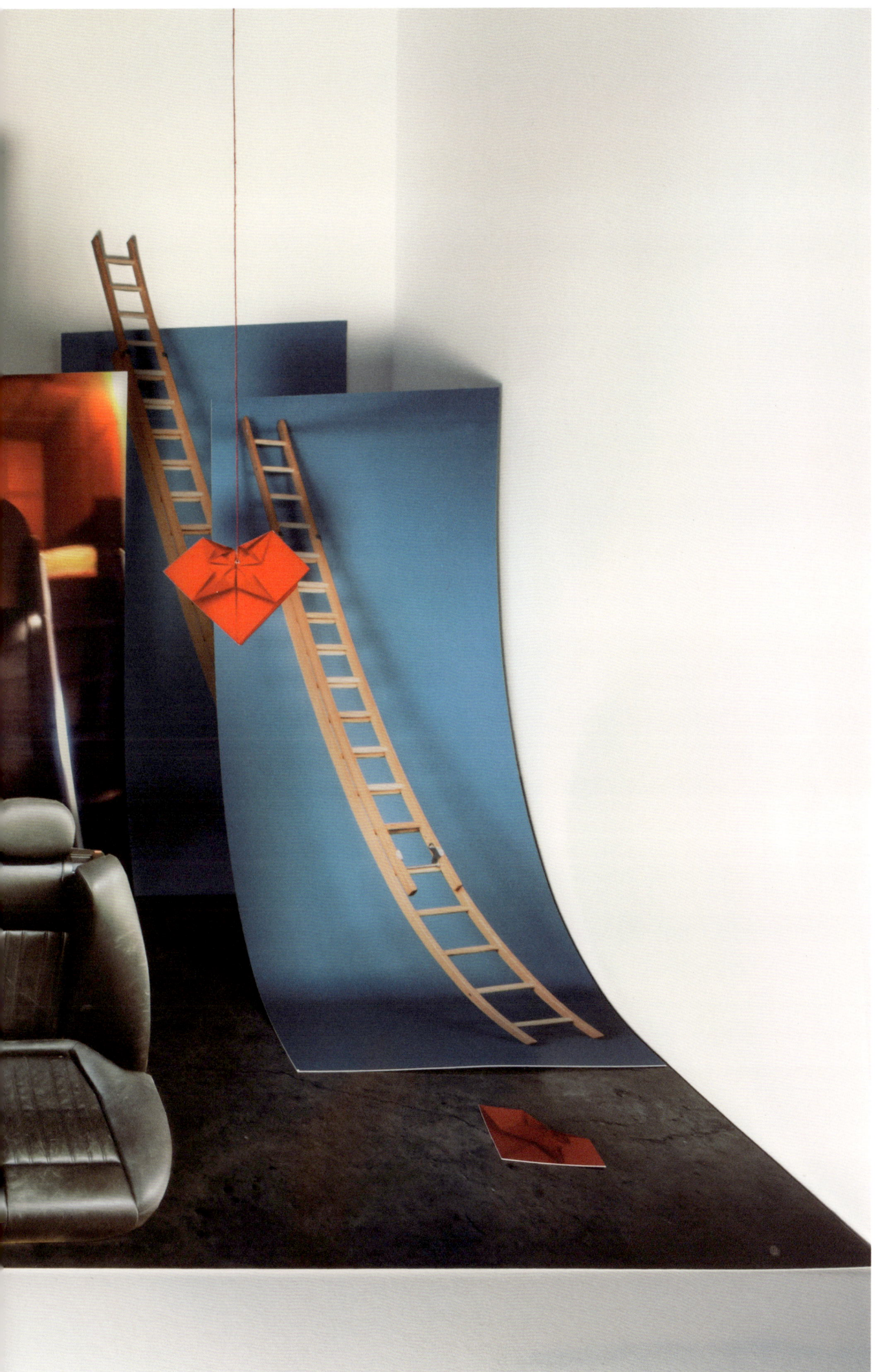

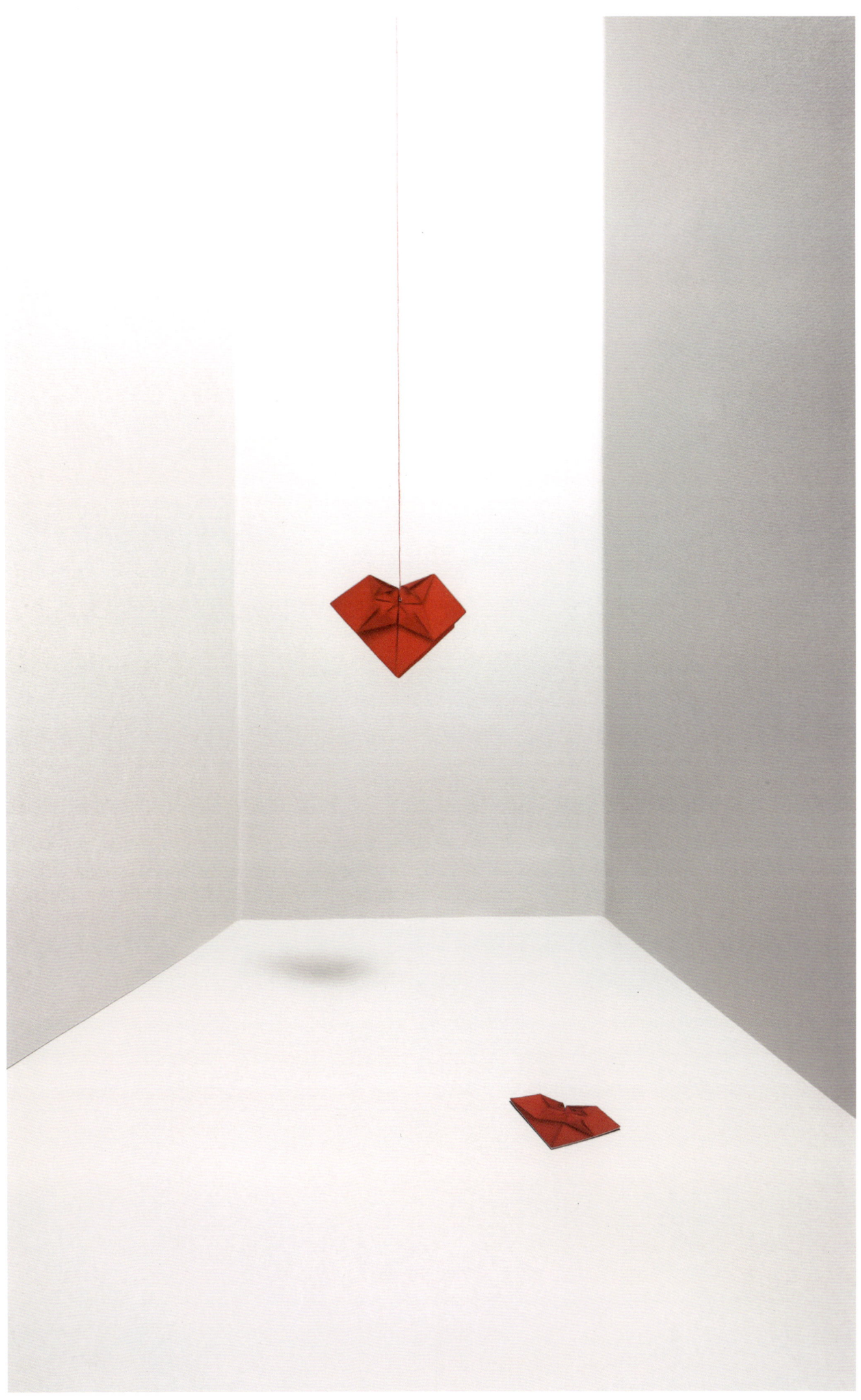

~~Daniel~~
~~Mason~~
~~Hudson~~
~~Spencer~~
~~Conor~~
~~Henry~~
~~Brandon~~
~~Pascal~~
~~Ray~~
~~Jimmy~~
~~Patrick~~
~~Kyle~~
~~Lee~~
~~Naomi~~
~~Kyle, again~~
~~Sam~~
~~Jack~~
~~Tony~~
~~Greg~~
~~Bennett~~
~~Charlie~~
~~Milo~~
~~Durant~~
~~Scott~~
~~Will~~
~~Durant, again~~
~~Nikolai~~
~~John~~
~~Carlos~~
~~Mike~~
~~Lukas~~

Will, again

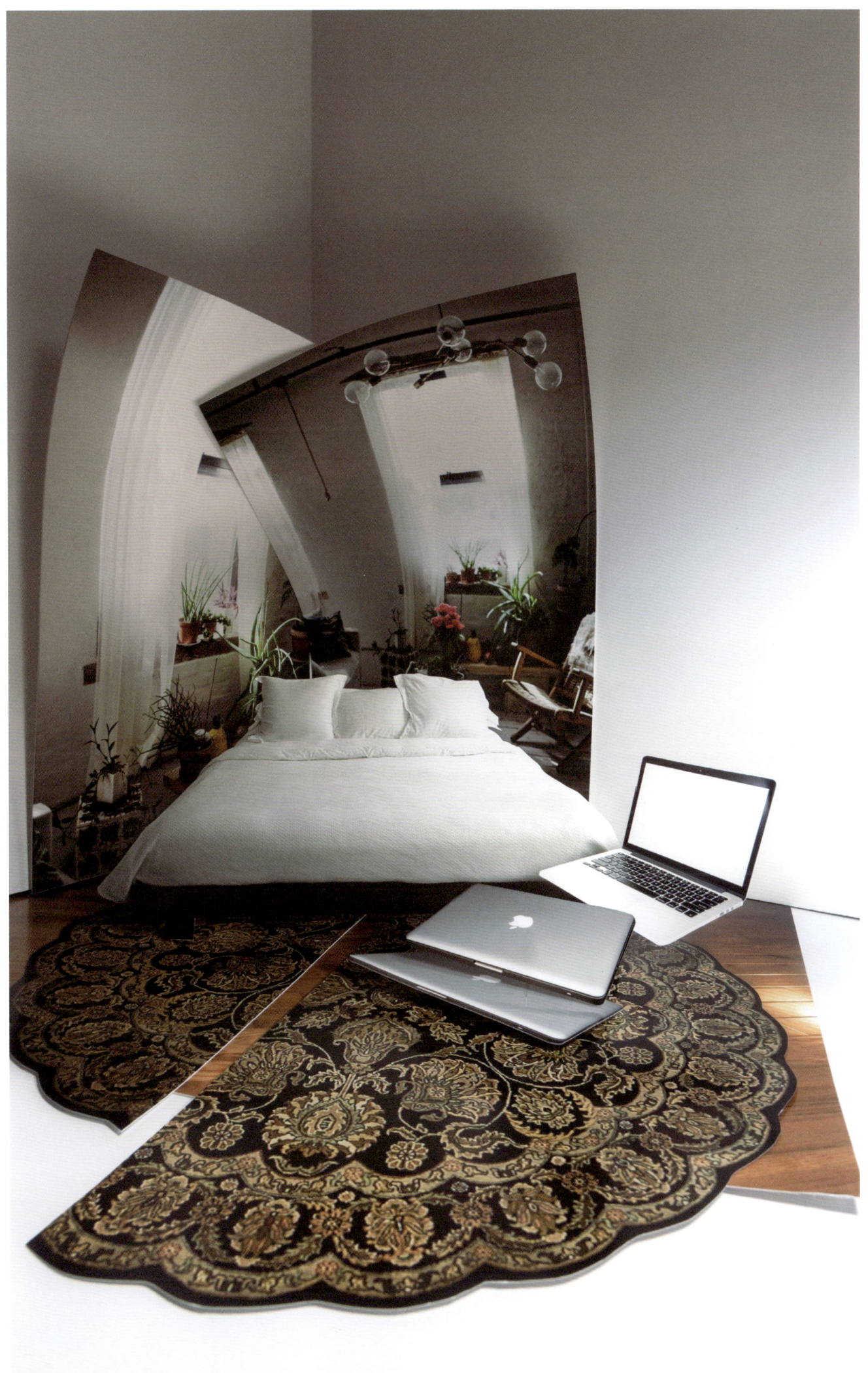

It had been two years since Will and I had stopped dating. We would see each other at a party or gallery sometimes and exchange small talk. It was uncomfortable, but not fraught. I had already had a long day by the time I saw Will's email. From the time stamp I knew that he was drunk. I read the whole thing over twice, trying to figure out what he was doing. He rambled in different directions: He didn't want there to be any hard feelings between us. He felt bad about not calling me. He was angry about that one time I was mean to his friends. He was seeing someone now. He needed me to know that.

I walked away from my computer and poured myself a drink. I paced my apartment, debating how to respond. I had another drink and considered moving to California. My radiator had been broken for months and I liked the idea of wearing thin shirts in November. I settled back in at my desk, typed one word and clicked send.

UNSUBSCRIBE.

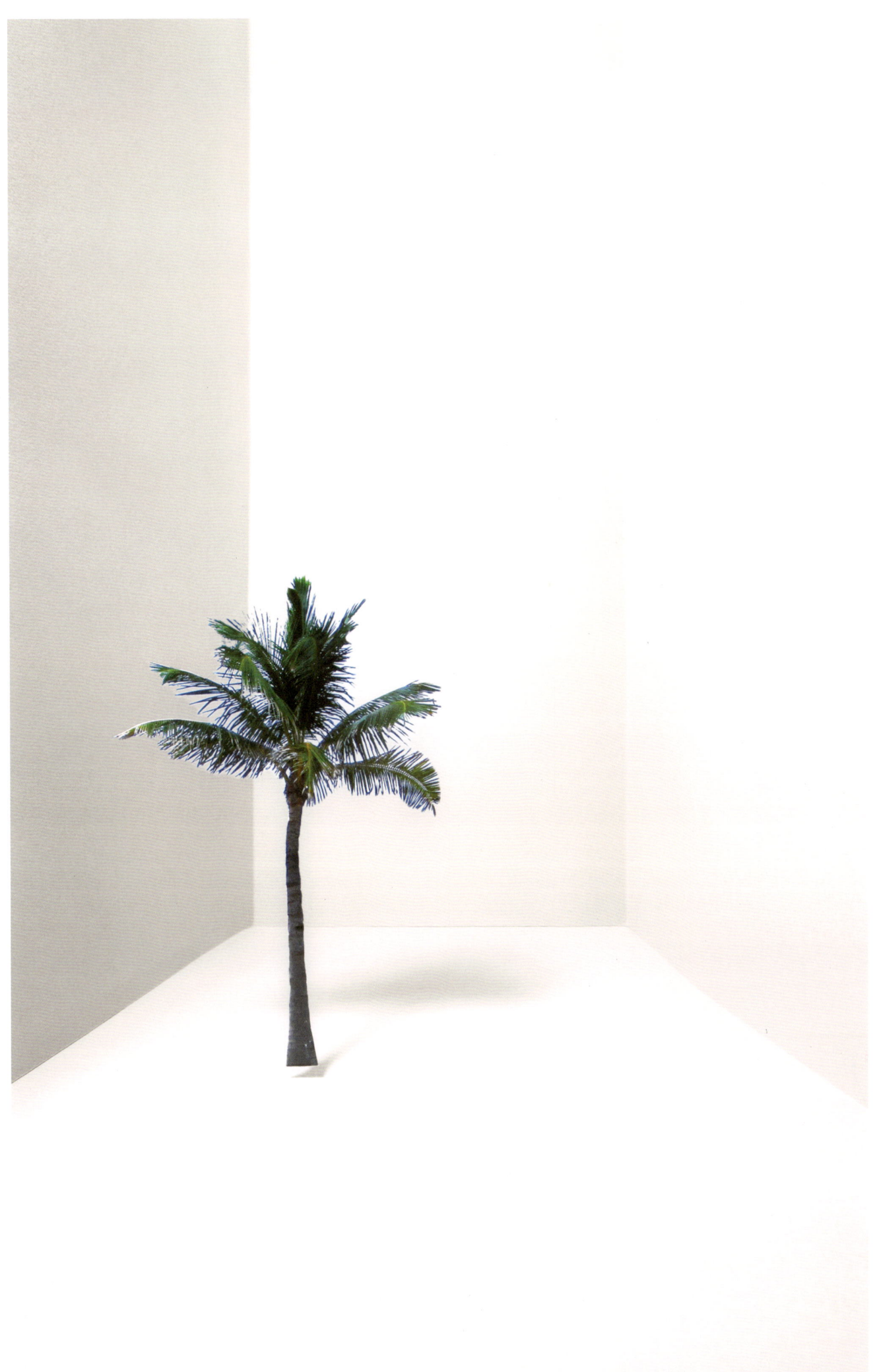

~~Daniel~~
~~Mason~~
~~Hudson~~
~~Spencer~~
~~Conor~~
~~Henry~~
~~Brandon~~
~~Pascal~~
~~Ray~~
~~Jimmy~~
~~Patrick~~
~~Kyle~~
~~Lee~~
~~Naomi~~
~~Kyle, again~~
~~Sam~~
~~Jack~~
~~Tony~~
~~Greg~~
~~Bennett~~
~~Charlie~~
~~Milo~~
~~Durant~~
~~Scott~~
~~Will~~
~~Durant, again~~
~~Nikolai~~
~~John~~
~~Carlos~~
~~Mike~~
~~Lukas~~
~~Will, again~~

Gunner

Gunner was older than me, but lived like an emancipated teenager. He was an animator on a popular TV show, which impressed me until he told me that it was the artistic equivalent of being a physical laborer. He had a panic attack on our first date. He let the registration on his truck expire. His bedroom had been taken over by his cat. I wasn't allowed to witness it for myself, but he told me that he slept on his living room couch. I had it in my head that relationships should be wrung dry—squeezed of any useful or fascinating bits—so I tried to stick it out. I forgave him for standing me up. My instinct to lie to my friends about him was just one more red flag that I ignored. He was tall. He said my name in a quiet, deep voice that shook me.

He called me one night, to talk about our relationship. He asked if I'd meet him for coffee and my first thought was that it wasn't worth putting on mascara. *Let's just talk on the phone*, I said, and from that moment on it was a race to see who could break up with who first. Gunner said that he hadn't thought that the age difference was going to matter much to him, but it did. I was just *too immature* for him. I heard a gurgling noise, followed by a sharp inhalation.

Are you smoking a bong?

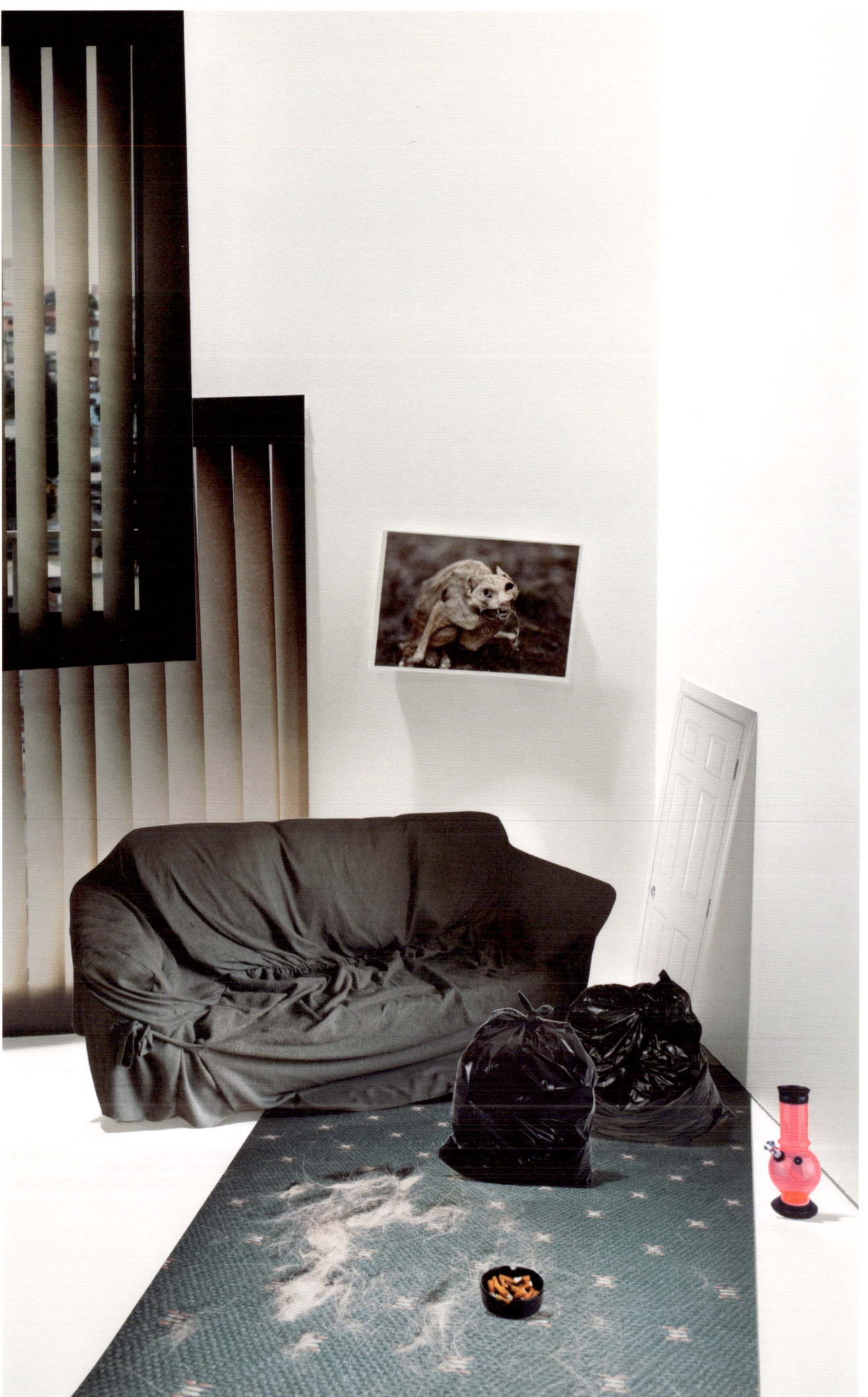

~~Daniel~~
~~Mason~~
~~Hudson~~
~~Spencer~~
~~Conor~~
~~Henry~~
~~Brandon~~
~~Pascal~~
~~Ray~~
~~Jimmy~~
~~Patrick~~
~~Kyle~~
~~Lee~~
~~Naomi~~
~~Kyle, again~~
~~Sam~~
~~Jack~~
~~Tony~~
~~Greg~~
~~Bennett~~
~~Charlie~~
~~Milo~~
~~Durant~~
~~Scott~~
~~Will~~
~~Durant, again~~
~~Nikolai~~
~~John~~
~~Carlos~~
~~Mike~~
~~Lukas~~
~~Will, again~~
~~Gunner~~

James

James should have been the one. He was good to animals. He picked me up in his station wagon at five a.m. when I called him crying. He cooked an entire seder with me, because I was using loose faith to cope with a breakup. He wrote me beautiful letters and introduced me to incredible music. We kissed each other's best friends but never each other. After a few years, there was a shift. I stopped asking about his love life. I stopped telling him about mine. I was ashamed of the guys that I slept with, not because James shamed me, but because they were garbage compared to him. When I got into James's car, I didn't want either of us to love anyone else.

We spent a week at a cabin on Lake Canandaigua. We grilled vegetables in our bathing suits. We watched movies that we bought for three dollars at a video store that was going out of business. Friends came and went, but James and I stayed the whole week. I imagined we were married and that our friends were our children. He wrapped his arms around me in front of the fire, but still, we slept in separate bedrooms.

We saw each other less and less. Our letters had become romantic. What had once felt holy between us was now a tether, holding each of us back.

We were at a party and hadn't seen each other in months. I drank too much on purpose. I did shots of whiskey, knowing that I was going to kiss him, and knowing that it might ruin everything. I told him that I loved him. I told him that I knew he loved me too. He didn't deny it. I laughed at how stupid we were. *This will never actually happen.* Too much time had gone by. I was too drunk to explain it well and I was angry that he'd never made a move. *I'm going home with someone else tonight,* was the last thing I said to him.

I've reached out to his closest friends, but no one's heard from him in years.

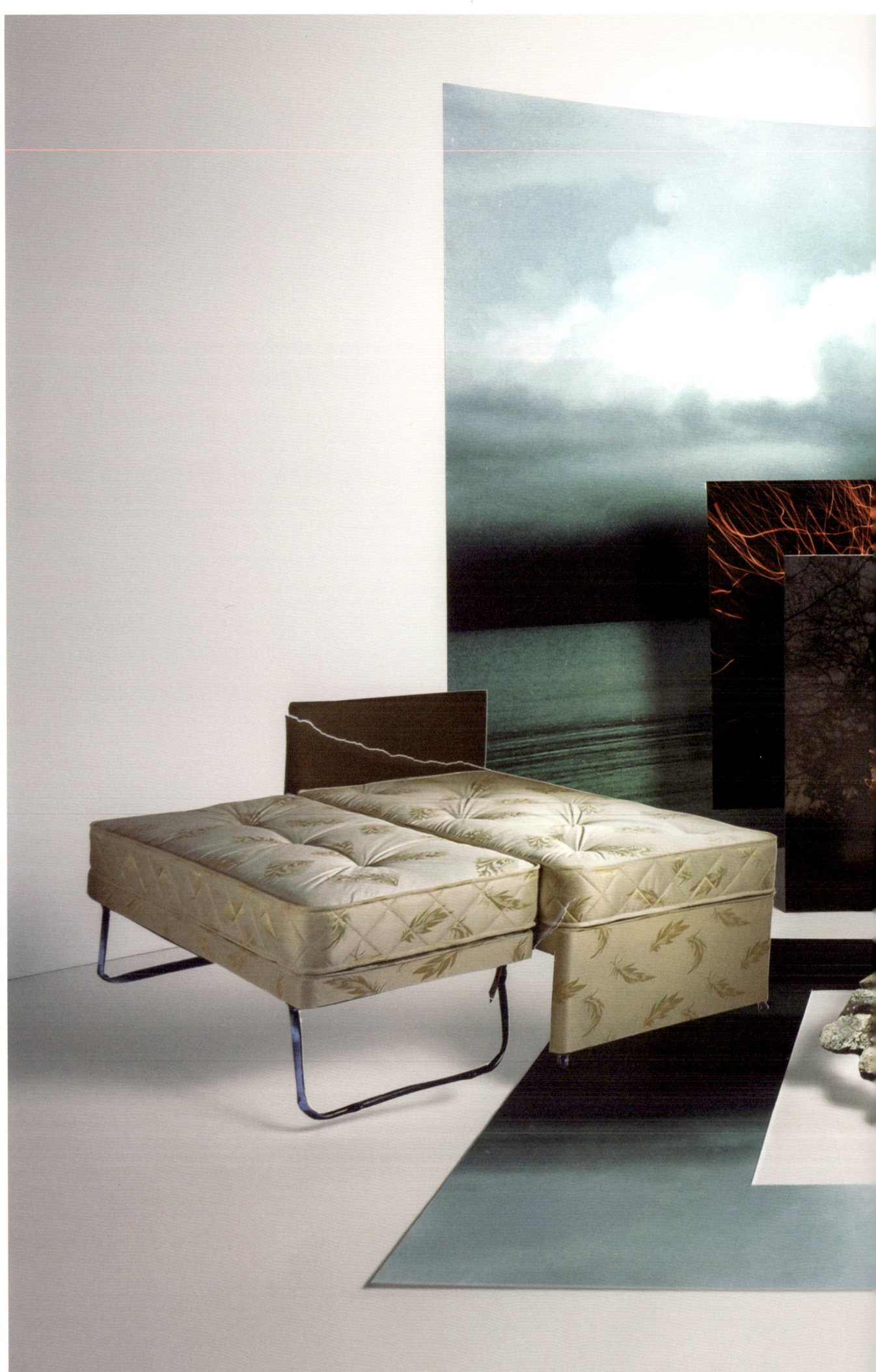

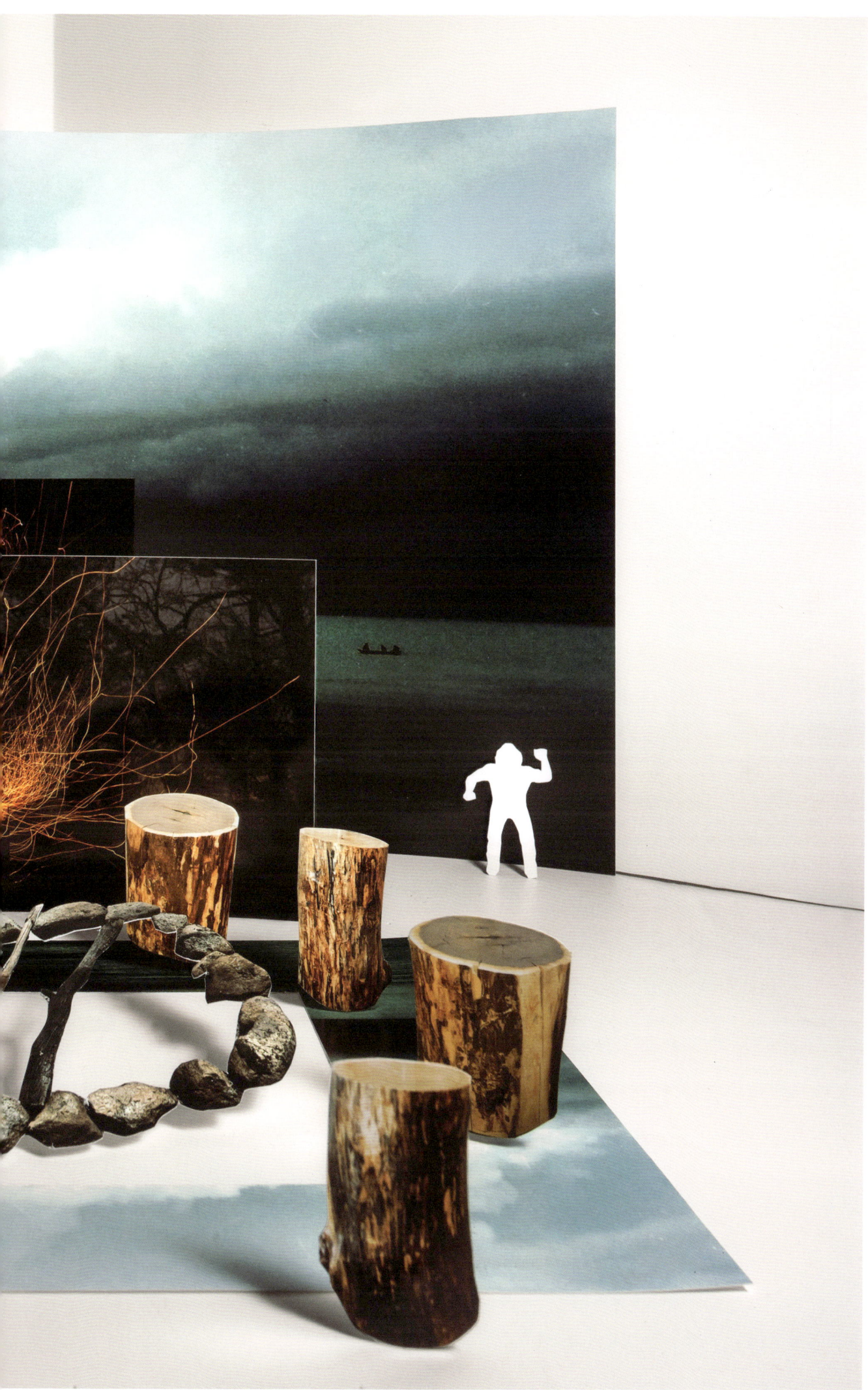

~~Daniel~~
~~Mason~~
~~Hudson~~
~~Spencer~~
~~Conor~~
Henry
Brandon
~~Pascal~~
~~Ray~~
~~Jimmy~~
Patrick
~~Kyle~~
~~Lee~~
Naomi
Kyle, again
Sam
~~Jack~~
~~Tony~~
Greg
Bennett
~~Charlie~~
Milo
~~Durant~~
~~Scott~~
Will
~~Durant, again~~
~~Nikolai~~
~~John~~
~~Carlos~~
Mike
~~Lukas~~
~~Will, again~~
~~Gunner~~
~~James~~

Adam

Adam and I had gotten together during a week that I was home, visiting. He kissed me in a basement bar and I fucked him in my parents' house, full of guests. Our bodies came naturally to one another. It surprised me. I had to leave town again and I meant to leave him alone, but I couldn't. We started emailing each other. We argued over television and movies. I watched things in order to have an excuse to email him. Presumably, we were both seeing other people, but he meant something to me.

On my next trip, we were only overlapping for one night, but we agreed to make it count. He was supposed to meet me at a friend's party. He delayed and delayed, finally showing up outside the bar at three a.m. We went straight home, but it wasn't like before. We kept misinterpreting each other, but still searched for a connection. We joked that we were both too fucked up to make anything work, but I still wanted to believe that the underlying message was, *If only we could.*

I'd only been asleep for a couple of hours when I woke up to Adam with his coat on, tying his shoes. He had clearly been hoping that I wouldn't catch him leaving.

This probably looks pretty bad, he said.

I think it looks great, was all I could think of to say, glaring.

I walked him downstairs, but kept my distance. I didn't understand what had happened, but I was angry about it. We stood awkwardly in the doorway, cold air blowing in. I kept my arms around myself and off him.

Later, I found out that his father was dying. None of it had anything to do with me. His heart had been breaking, but all I'd been able to see was my own disappointment.

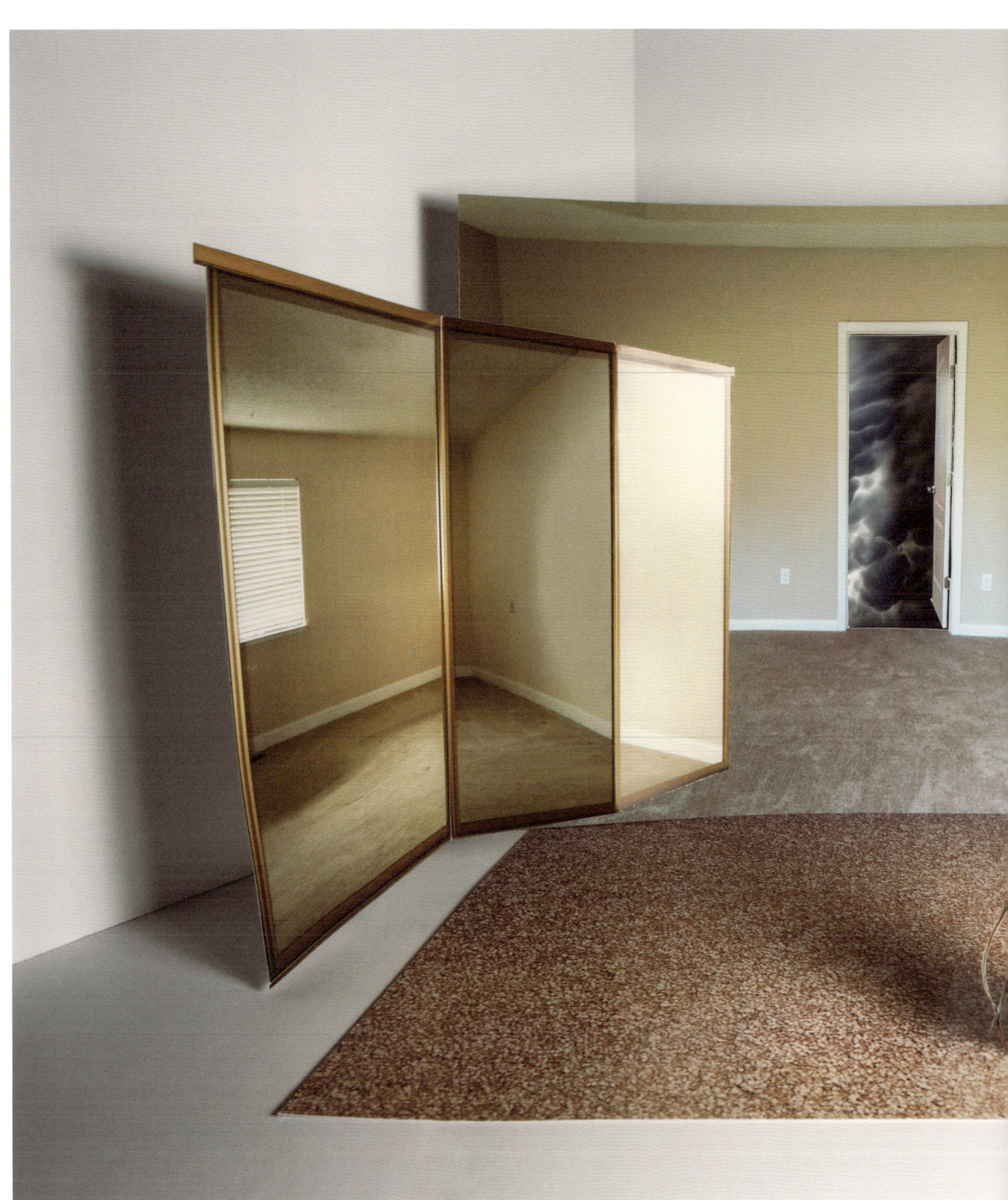

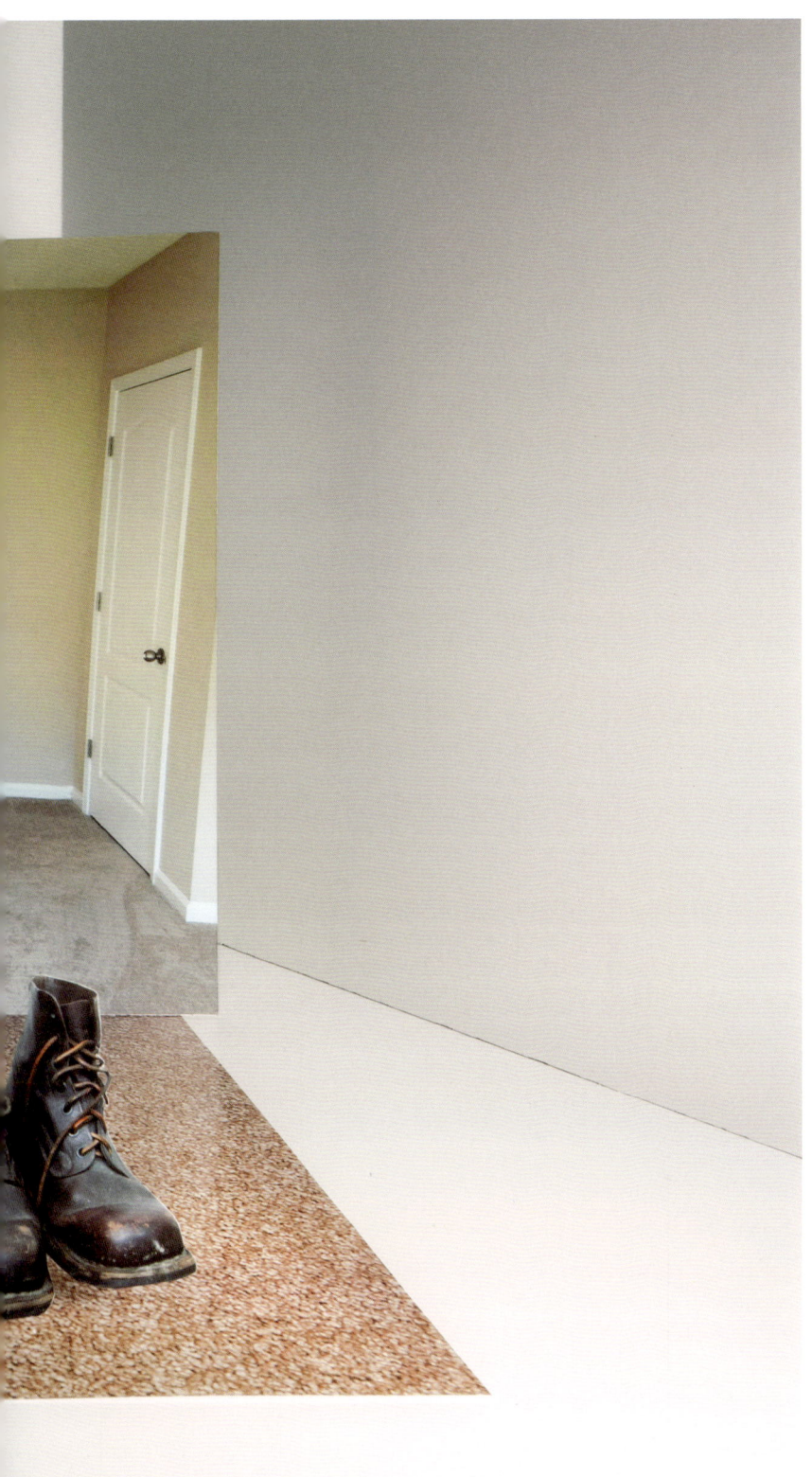

~~Daniel~~
~~Mason~~
~~Hudson~~
~~Spencer~~
~~Conor~~
~~Henry~~
~~Brandon~~
~~Pascal~~
~~Ray~~
~~Jimmy~~
~~Patrick~~
~~Kyle~~
~~Lee~~
~~Naomi~~
~~Kyle, again~~
~~Sam~~
~~Jack~~
~~Tony~~
~~Greg~~
~~Bennett~~
~~Charlie~~
~~Milo~~
~~Durant~~
~~Scott~~
~~Will~~
~~Durant, again~~
~~Nikolai~~
~~John~~
~~Carlos~~
~~Mike~~
~~Lukas~~
~~Will, again~~
~~Gunner~~
~~James~~
~~Adam~~

Caleb

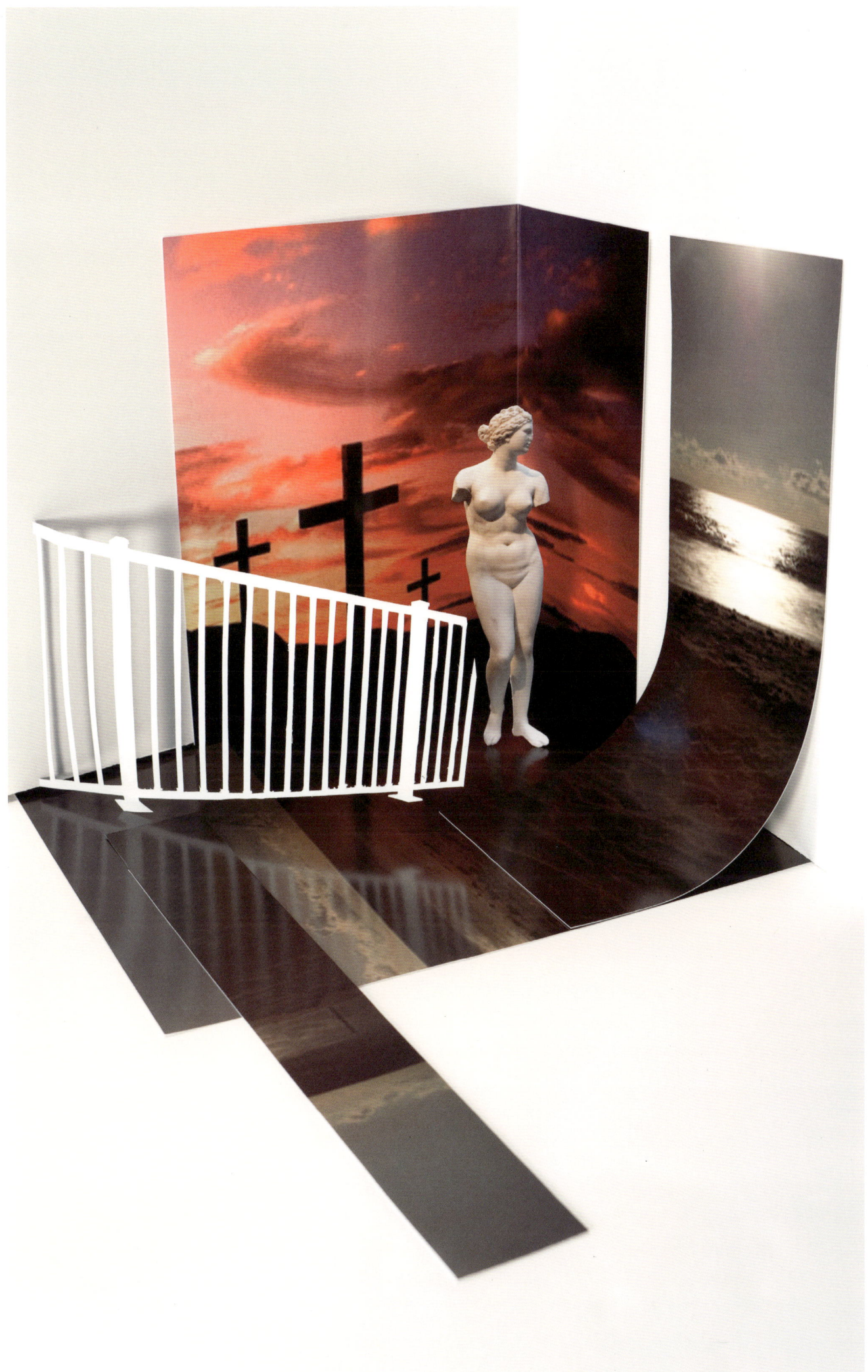

Caleb and I were near the beach. The bar had been too loud, but neither of us was ready to make a move. We found a spot with a view. He confessed that he'd been married, when he was a teenager. He told me that they were Christian and that, before their wedding day, they'd never kissed. He'd taught Sunday school. That was ten years ago. Now he was divorced, getting a PhD in film studies. He hesitated over the religion question before explaining that he'd moved away from *all that*, although he still considered himself *spiritual*.

I pushed against a metal railing. Caleb stood behind me and commented on the ocean, my hair, their smells. He was becoming sentimental. He was trying to figure out a way to get me to come home with him. I'd been planning on it the whole time, but he didn't know that. The sentimentality stopped me, though. It felt like emotional foreplay, for his benefit and not mine. He was tricking himself into thinking he really cared about me. It felt like he was laying the groundwork for how he would later justify to himself the casual fucking of an atheist Jewess.

When I told him that I wouldn't go home with him—wouldn't meet his dog or check out his DVDs or whatever bullshit he was trying to work with—he seemed relieved. And I was too, because there's nothing like a former Sunday school teacher to make you feel like a whore.

~~Daniel~~
~~Mason~~
~~Hudson~~
~~Spencer~~
~~Conor~~
~~Henry~~
~~Brandon~~
~~Pascal~~
~~Ray~~
~~Jimmy~~
~~Patrick~~
~~Kyle~~
~~Lee~~
~~Naomi~~
~~Kyle, again~~
~~Sam~~
~~Jack~~
~~Tony~~
~~Greg~~
~~Bennett~~
~~Charlie~~
~~Milo~~
~~Durant~~
~~Scott~~
~~Will~~
~~Durant, again~~
~~Nikolai~~
~~John~~
~~Carlos~~
~~Mike~~
~~Lukas~~
~~Will, again~~
~~Gunner~~
~~James~~
~~Adam~~
~~Caleb~~

Owen

Owen had a job that brought him to California for the summer, where I was living. We were friends from college, but he'd grown up since then. He was working on a boat. His shoulders were broad. He made me laugh more deeply than anyone ever had.

During that summer, Owen admitted that he'd had a crush on me in college, which I'd known but enjoyed hearing. When I asked him why, he said my full name as though it held some power. I wondered what it was exactly that I represented to him. Whatever it was, it seemed to feel out of reach to him. I was still hoping that we might have some future, but he didn't believe that I'd ever stick with him. He was probably right.

He watched me while I put on lotion and got dressed. He smiled. *Whatever you do, when it's over, please don't give me the whole "I just can't do this anymore" line.*

Oh, I said, putting my shirt on. *How about, "It's over"?*

Yeah, he said, pulling me back. *But not yet.*

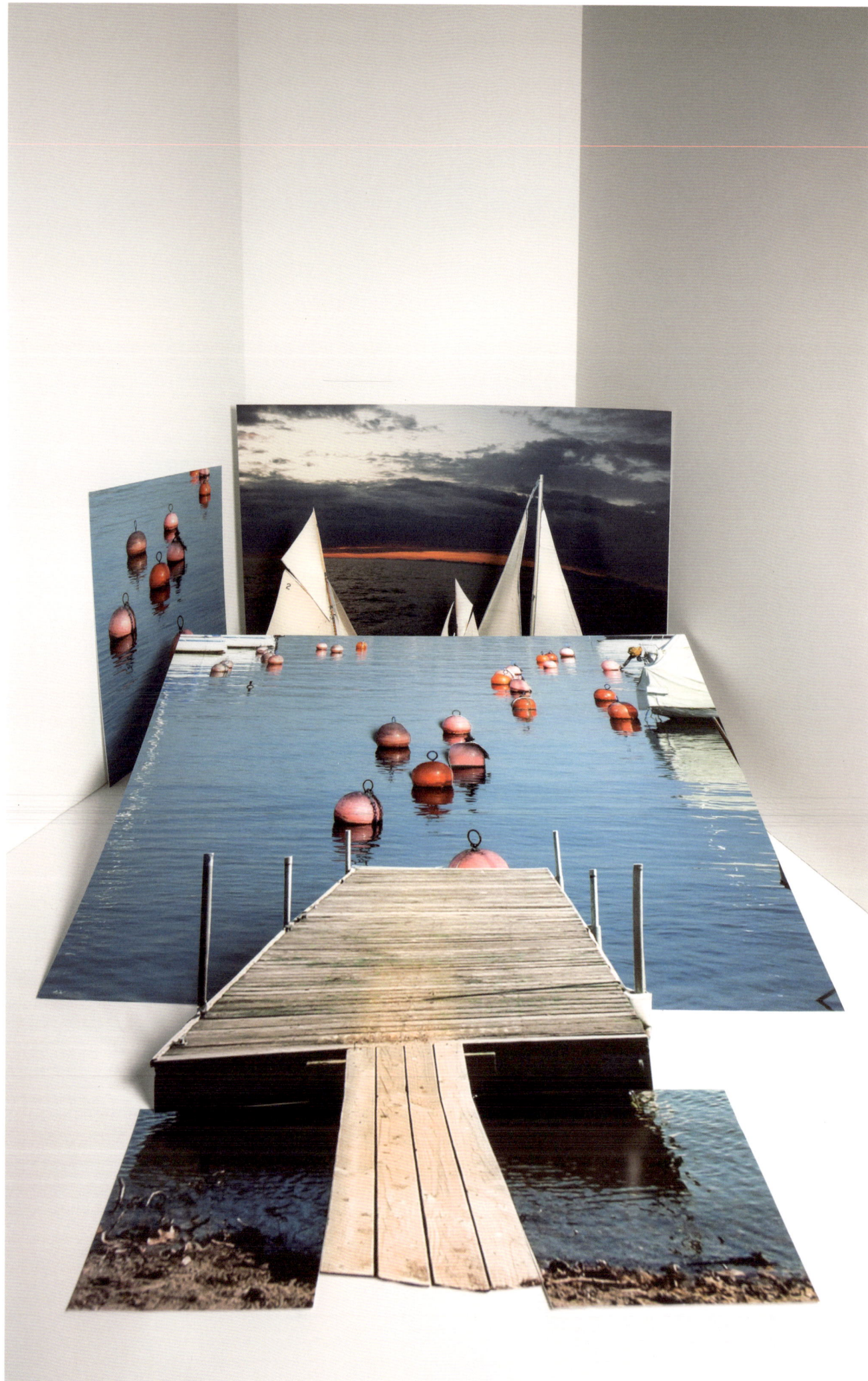

~~Daniel~~
~~Mason~~
~~Hudson~~
~~Spencer~~
~~Conor~~
~~Henry~~
~~Brandon~~
~~Pascal~~
~~Ray~~
~~Jimmy~~
~~Patrick~~
~~Kyle~~
~~Lee~~
~~Naomi~~
~~Kyle, again~~
~~Sam~~
~~Jack~~
~~Tony~~
~~Greg~~
~~Bennett~~
~~Charlie~~
~~Milo~~
~~Durant~~
~~Scott~~
~~Will~~
~~Durant, again~~
~~Nikolai~~
~~John~~
~~Carlos~~
~~Mike~~
~~Lukas~~
~~Will, again~~
~~Gunner~~
~~James~~
~~Adam~~
~~Caleb~~
~~Owen~~

Sam, again

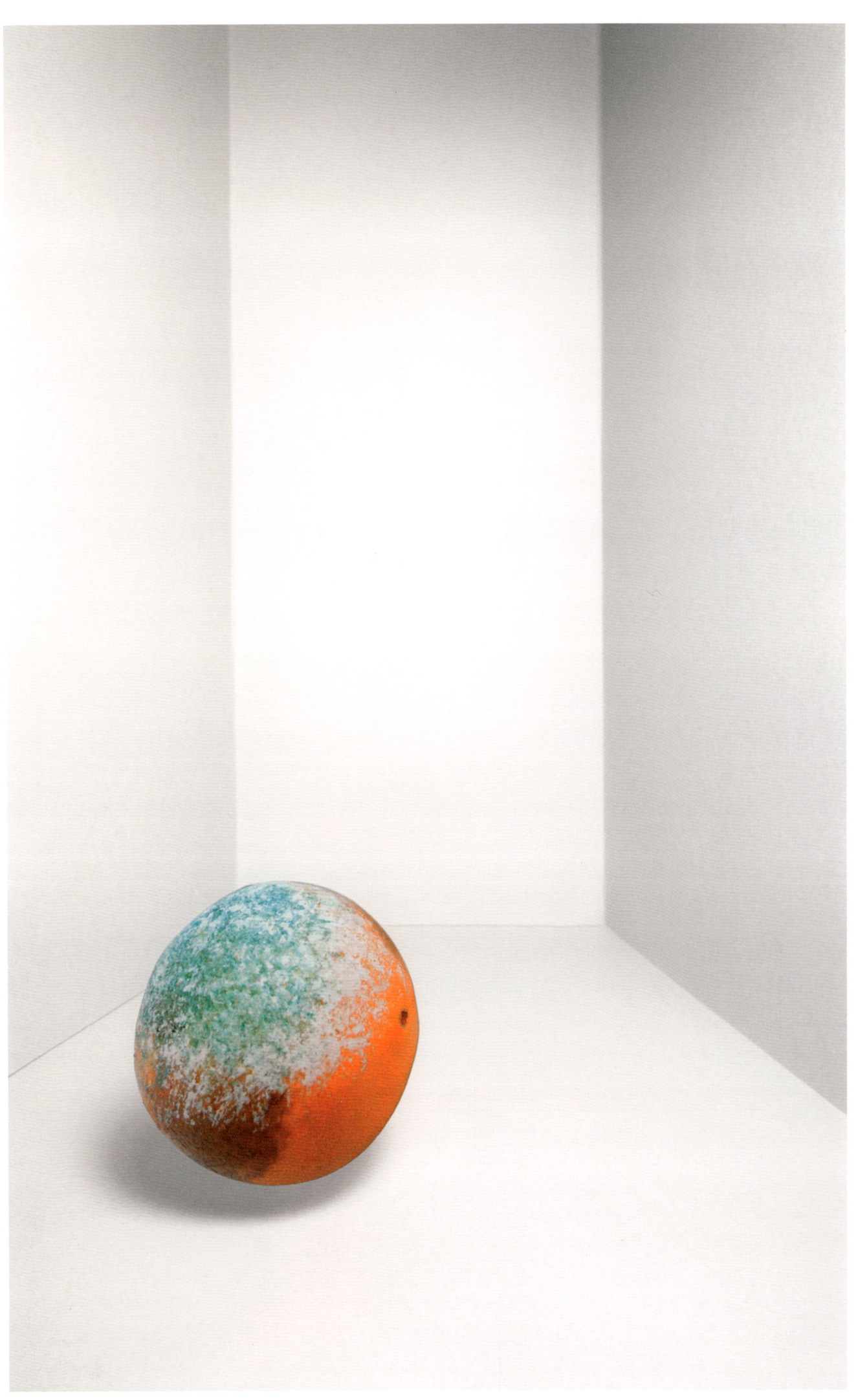

At first we had excuses for the calls. Then, we didn't. We felt as though we had a right to one another, even when we were involved with other people. He'd had a girlfriend for years, but I never thought about her. I couldn't.

Sam called me from a bathroom at a bachelor party. He heard my breath catch and quickly assured me that he wasn't the groom. *Not yet.* He asked me what I was wearing, but I wouldn't answer. He apologized and I forgave him.

I was so mean to you back then, I said.

I love you, he said.

The next time he called me, we were both drunk, time zones apart. *They treated us badly so now we behave badly. You see that, don't you?* Sam didn't answer. Instead, he asked me again what I was wearing. He asked if I remembered the time on the floor. *I had rug burns for two years*, I told him.

Tell me about it, he said. *Slowly.*

Neither of us were feeling much else. I never knew if it was only revenge. We were both trying to erase them for one another. I think it worked a little.

That's not what I meant, he said, *but it was just like that.*

I took a cab home with my cell phone tucked into my bra. The ride was smooth, all through the canyons and into the valley. The driver told me that he saw a mountain lion once. In exchange, I told him that I was involved with someone else's boyfriend. *Neither of us are good people. We feel like we have a free pass to behave this way, but we don't. Do we?*

No free pass, the driver said. I knew that he only meant the ride, but I pretended he meant more. I put my phone into my purse and faced the window, looking for lions.

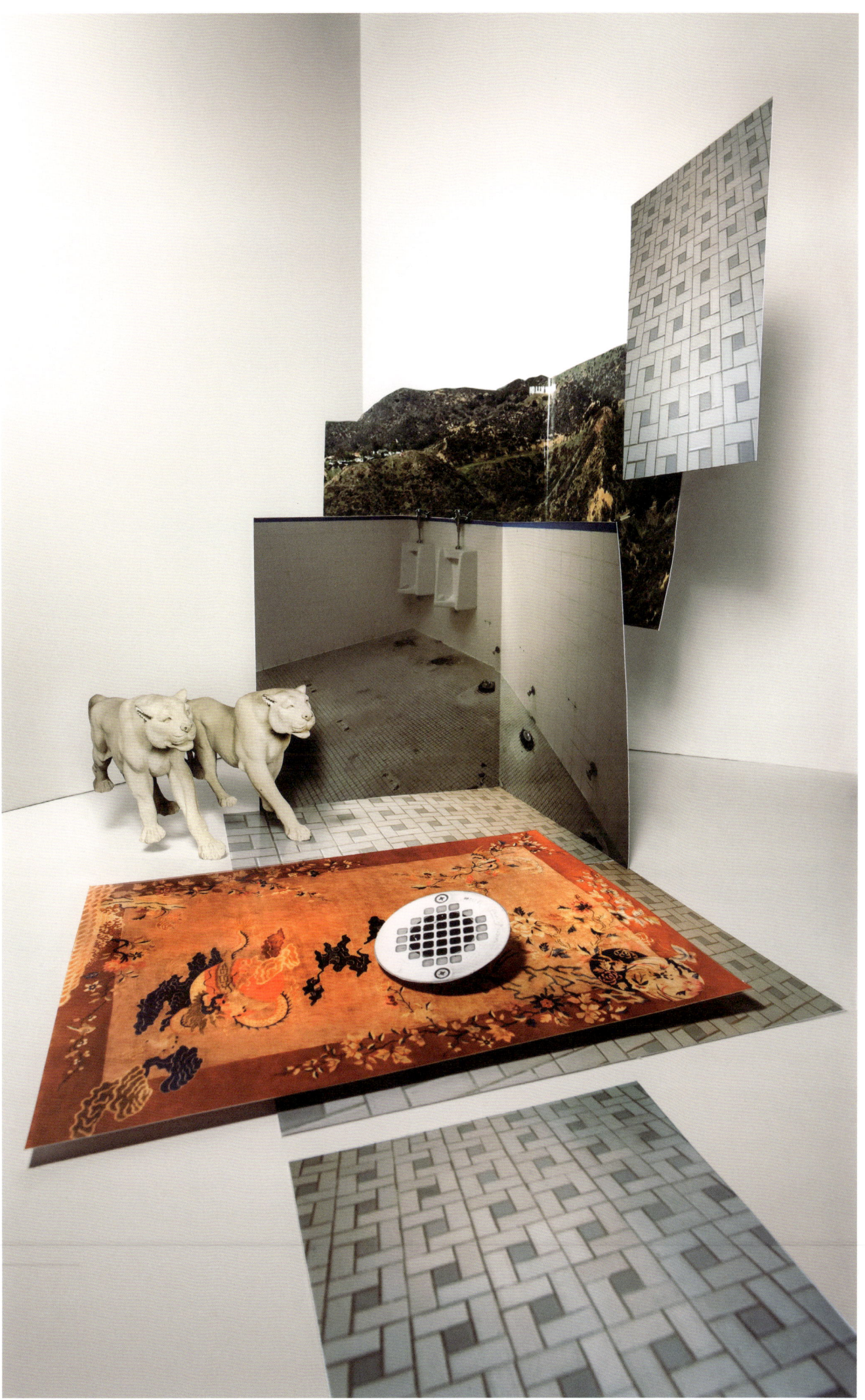

~~Daniel~~
~~Mason~~
~~Hudson~~
~~Spencer~~
~~Conor~~
Henry
Brandon
~~Pascal~~
~~Ray~~
~~Jimmy~~
Patrick
~~Kyle~~
~~Lee~~
~~Naomi~~
~~Kyle, again~~
~~Sam~~
~~Jack~~
~~Tony~~
~~Greg~~
Bennett
~~Charlie~~
Milo
~~Durant~~
~~Scott~~
~~Will~~
~~Durant, again~~
Nikolai
~~John~~
~~Carlos~~
Mike
~~Lukas~~
~~Will, again~~
~~Gunner~~
James
~~Adam~~
~~Caleb~~
~~Owen~~
~~Sam, again~~

Chase

Chase had picked me up at an oyster bar where I was working. I think he was on mushrooms, but I gave him my number anyway. He had made money selling face masks during an avian flu epidemic. He didn't seem to know what to do with himself after that. He squeezed his eyes shut a lot, which always made him look like he was just waking up.

He told me he was going to cook me dinner. It put me off when I got to his apartment and realized that he was making soup. Serge Gainsbourg was playing loudly through expensive speakers. I tried to enjoy myself. I drank most of the bottle of wine that I had brought, while Chase smoked an entire joint. The soup took forever and needed salt, but I reminded myself that he was trying.

We had sex afterwards, which I guess is the whole point of not going to a restaurant. He brought out his laptop after, asking if I wanted to watch something. I told him to put on whatever he wanted. He chose *Ren and Stimpy* from his recently watched list and almost immediately started laughing along. I got hung up on his weird pretentious taste in music mixed with his lowbrow taste in television. I realized I didn't understand a single thing about him, and the idea of spending the night made me panic. He was hurt when I said that I wanted to sleep in my own bed, but I didn't care.

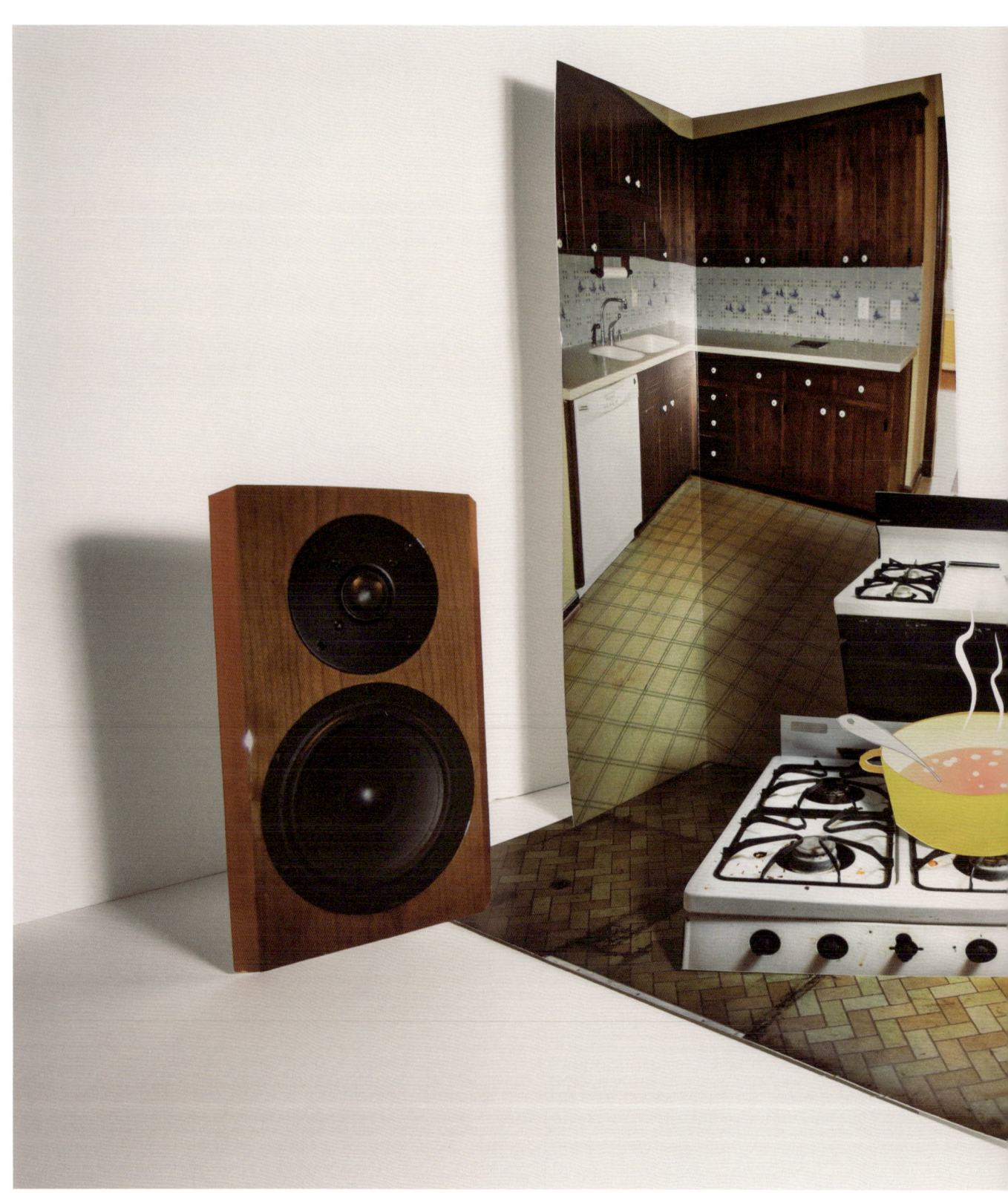

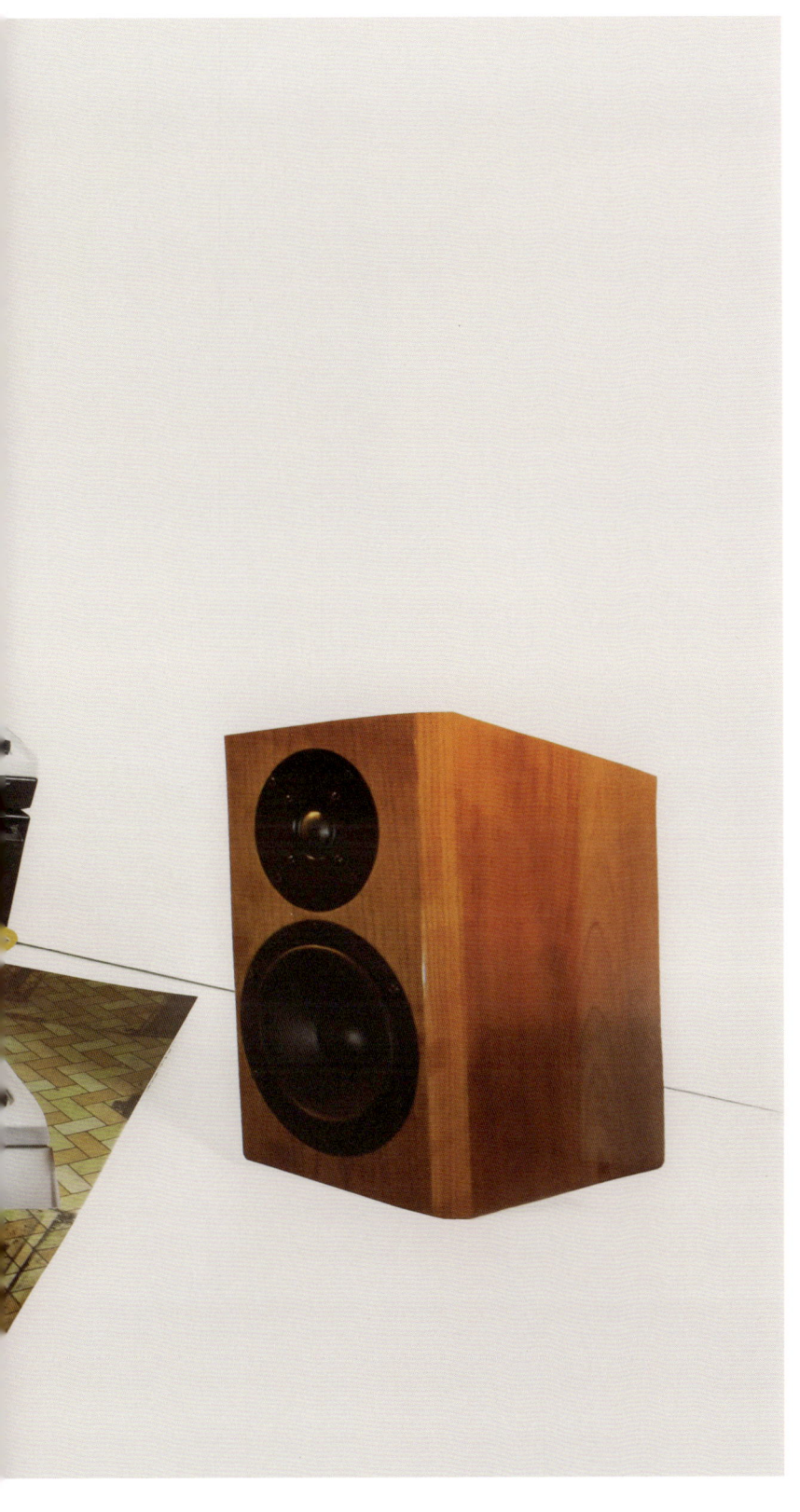

~~Daniel~~
~~Mason~~
~~Hudson~~
~~Spencer~~
~~Conor~~
~~Henry~~
~~Brandon~~
~~Pascal~~
~~Ray~~
~~Jimmy~~
~~Patrick~~
~~Kyle~~
~~Lee~~
~~Naomi~~
~~Kyle, again~~
~~Sam~~
~~Jack~~
~~Tony~~
~~Greg~~
~~Bennett~~
~~Charlie~~
~~Milo~~
~~Durant~~
~~Scott~~
~~Will~~
~~Durant, again~~
~~Nikolai~~
~~John~~
~~Carlos~~
~~Mike~~
~~Lukas~~
~~Will, again~~
~~Gunner~~
~~James~~
~~Adam~~
~~Caleb~~
~~Owen~~
~~Sam, again~~
~~Chase~~

Asher

Asher was an adult—a lawyer. He owned his apartment, picked great restaurants and showed up on time. When I told him that I hadn't filed taxes in two years, Asher said he would help. I tried to make it work because, in a lot of ways, he was what I needed. He was stable. I was flighty, but he never seemed to mind when I had to shift plans at the last minute.

It was wrong from the beginning. We had connected through a website that I couldn't take seriously. His emails had been overly earnest. Before our first date, I waited outside the restaurant picking at my cuticles and feeling dread creep up my legs.

I couldn't relax. We were in a gastropub with beautiful subway tiles. I kept thinking that I knew the people sitting at other tables—old college roommates, friends of my parents. The idea of introducing Asher to anyone made me anxious. He wasn't cool. He had a parrot and very few friends. I stayed with him for a little while, convincing myself that this was what growing up was but, everywhere we went, I worried about being seen.

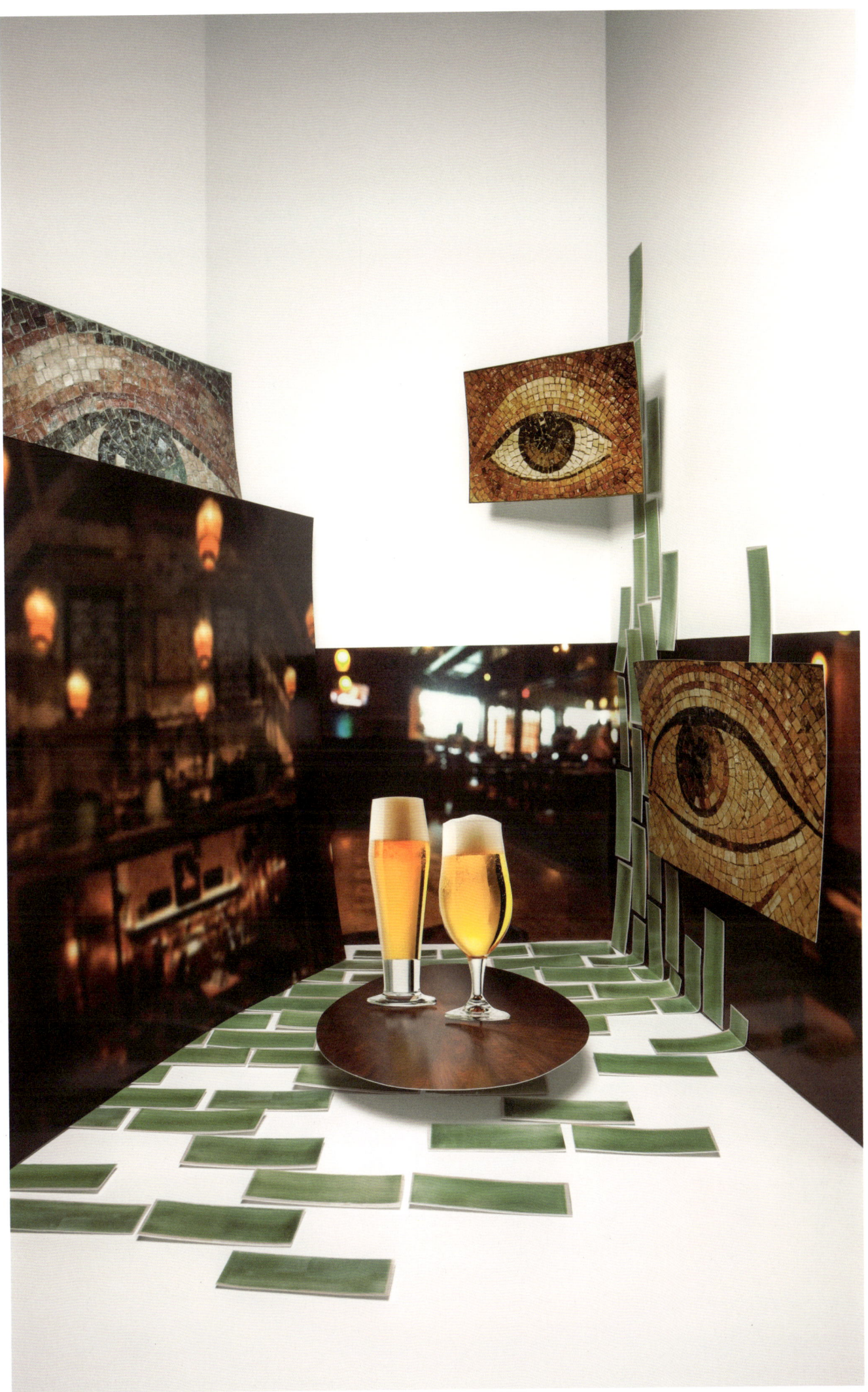

Daniel
Mason
Hudson
Spencer
Conor
Henry
Brandon
Pascal
Ray
Jimmy
Patrick
Kyle
Lee
Naomi
Kyle, again
Sam
Jack
Tony
Greg
Bennett
Charlie
Milo
Durant
Scott
Will
Durant, again
Nikolai
John
Carlos
Mike
Lukas
Will, again
Gunner
James
Adam
Caleb
Owen
Sam, again
Chase
Asher

Theo

Theo was the first person to like the things about me that I liked about myself. It made me feel seen and hungry. The windows of his bedroom looked out over canyons. I watched the lights of the observatory while he went down on me and tried to push out the thought that I couldn't hold on to that moment forever. From the very beginning, I felt love swelling in my chest, but fear swelled right beside it. I dreaded each day, knowing it might be the one to reveal the inevitable thing that would make one of us unlovable. I can say with full certainty that I was never as scared in my entire life.

The first night we spent together, he never took his hands off me. If he ever had, I might have left. I knew that if I woke up beside him, I'd be done. And I was. The sun came up and I thought to myself, *This has to be my life. It has to be with him.* Before getting dressed, I rubbed Theo's elbow while he told me his dreams. He had discovered me on a bed of larvae, surrounded by enormous robotic spiders. *They were going to kill you. I wasn't doing anything about it. I didn't help you.* He felt terrible. I reminded him that I was fine, when really, all I thought was, *Yes. This is it. No one can help me.*

I began to feel like the shaky addicts in church basements, telling myself to take it one day at a time. I tried to swallow whole each moment that pushed me deeper and deeper into Theo: His stricken face the first time I got mad. The care he took when he pricked my arm, testing my blood sugar. The fact that he never lost his humor—not even during sex.

At night, I can feel it all threatening to come up. Each moment that I cling to sits hunched in my chest, quivering. I pray to a god that I don't believe in, wanting someone to assure me that these moments will be more than just that. I want to believe this will be a life and not just a story with a sad ending. I watch Theo sleep and have to stop myself from whispering my secrets into his waved hair:

I love you. It's killing me.

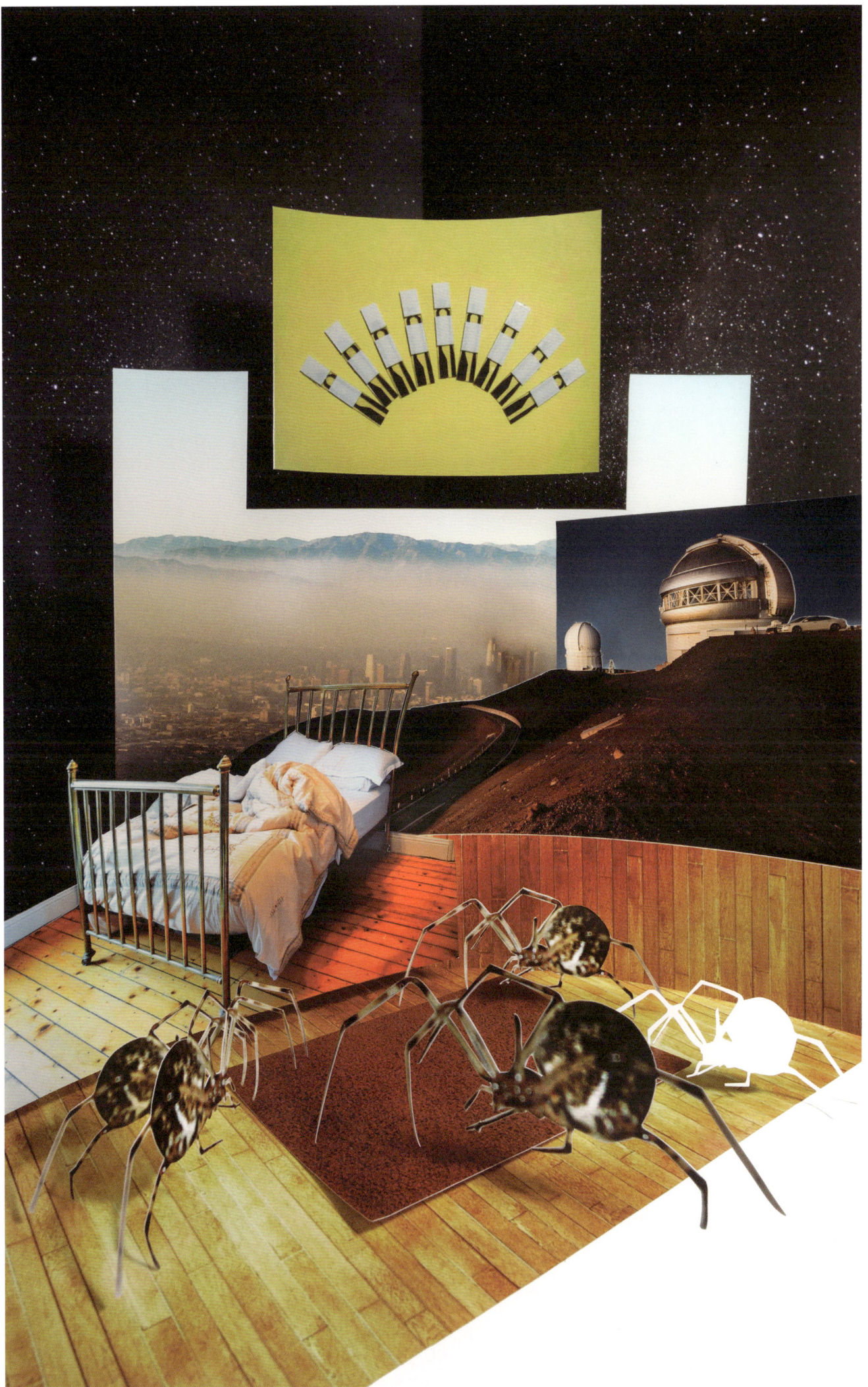